Praise for Richard Ryan's Holmes' tales

"The Vatican Cameos"

Winner of the Underground Book Reviews 'Novel of The Year – Readers Choice Award.'

Winner Silver Medal in the Readers' Favor͏ ok award contest.

"['The Vatican Cameos' ͏ ed and beautifully written Holme ͏ Times Bestselling author and the c͏

"Once you've read 'The Vat ͏ ͏ameos,' you'll find yourself eagerly awaiting the next in Ryan's series." – Fran Wood, What Fran's Reading for nj.com

"Richard T. Ryan's The Vatican Cameos is an excellent pastiche-length novel, very much in the spirit of the original Holmes stories by Sir Arthur Conan Doyle." – Dan Andriacco, author of a host of Holmes' tales as well as the blog, bakerstreetbest.com

"Loved it! A must read for all fans of Sherlock Holmes!" – Bits about Books

"Richard Ryan channels Dan Brown as well as Conan Doyle in this successful novel." – Tom Turley, Sherlockian author

"If you enjoy deeply researched historical fiction, combined with not one but two mystery/thriller stories, then you will really enjoy this excellent Sherlock Holmes pastiche." – Craig Copland, author of New Sherlock Holmes Mysteries

"A great addition to the Holmes Canon. Definitely worth a read." – Rob Hart, author of the Ash McKenna series

Preface

10 June, 1910

More than a decade has passed since the strange and tragic events that gripped the nation in 1899. In his long and storied career, I believe that these events constituted, without a doubt, one of the more unusual cases in which Sherlock Holmes ever became involved.

Much of the story has been withheld due to a certain sense of propriety and the abhorrence that both Holmes and I share with regard to scandal.

However, the real reason that the case was never published is quite simply because Holmes forbade it. In retrospect, I can understand his feelings on that matter. I have often written of my friend's vanity, perhaps his greatest weakness.

This case was one in which Holmes labored mightily, but with so few clues at his disposal, it was one in which he ultimately felt that he had not covered himself in glory. In fact, his exertions were such that at one point I even toyed with the idea of titling the work *Holmes Agonisties*.

Although I vehemently disagreed with him then (and I still do), I was not about to let the publication of such events drive a wedge between us. I valued Holmes' friendship far more than the few pounds I might have made from their publication.

Still, I think this adventure demonstrates all the better qualities that make up Sherlock Holmes – tenacity, ingenuity, brilliance and, dare I say it, compassion – and that they can be seen shining brightly through the otherwise sordid events.

And so, as always, the choice falls to someone other than I to make the decision as to the disposition of this work.

Those who have admired Holmes may want to honor his wish and perhaps re-read one of my other efforts. To quote Geoffrey Chaucer, you may feel free to *"Turne over the leef and chese another tale."*

However, I believe that those who choose that course will deprive themselves of as fine an exhibition of deductive prowess and wide-ranging knowledge as it has ever been my privilege to witness and chronicle.

Sincerely yours,

John H. Watson

"Noli tubare circulos meos!"

(Do not disturb my circles!)

Some believe these to be the last words of the Greek scientist and thinker, Archimedes

Chapter One – London, 1899

After a rather unremarkable winter, marked by a conspicuous absence of storms, during which Holmes and I were kept exceedingly busy, spring appeared to arrive early in 1899. By the second week of March, it had grown unseasonably warm, and I was beginning to think that crime had decided to take a holiday to celebrate the end of winter.

On Monday, the 20th, spring officially arrived without any undue fanfare. The day was rather mild and sunny, but otherwise, like the winter that had preceded it, totally without distinction. I say that because I remember distinctly that it passed without incident. In retrospect, I now realize that it truly was the calm before the storm.

The next morning, I awoke to discover Holmes had gone out early. When she brought my breakfast, Mrs. Hudson informed me that Inspector Lestrade had arrived at about seven o'clock and awakened her and Holmes in that order.

With nothing else to occupy my time and no word from my friend, I spent the day seeing a few patients and catching up on my correspondence. I ate a solitary dinner as Holmes had yet to return. After my meal, I visited my club, and when I returned to Baker Street, it was to an empty sitting room.

I was somewhat surprised – although not totally – at having no communication from Holmes.

I was just preparing to douse the lights and turn in when I heard my friend's familiar tread on the stairs. As he entered, I could tell by the dour expression on his face that something was terribly amiss. "What's wrong, Holmes?"

"It's a very bad business, Watson," he said rather sternly, shaking his head. "Very bad, indeed!"

"Where have you been all day, and what on Earth has happened?"

He replied, "I have spent the entire morning traveling and the better part of the afternoon at Stonehenge and have only just returned from Salisbury."

"What in heaven's name were you doing there?"

"Lestrade arrived shortly after the sun had risen this morning and had Mrs. Hudson rouse me from my bed. He then informed me that a ritual murder of some sort had been reported at Stonehenge. Since the local constabulary had requested that Scotland Yard look into the matter, he asked if I would be kind enough to accompany him."

"And what did you discover?"

"We arrived about midday and made our way to the site, which was now ringed with officers. On one of the smaller stones that might be said to resemble an altar, lay the naked body of a young woman. When I arrived, she had been covered by a sheet. If I were to guess, I would say that she was of average height, perhaps 140 pounds, with well-developed leg muscles and a head of ash blonde hair. A glance revealed that she had died from a single stab wound to the heart, after which she had been eviscerated.

"Her organs had been carefully arranged around the body, and her own blood had been used to paint a number of symbols on various parts of her body. Above her head and at both her sides were branches that had been cut from a yew tree. They had obviously been positioned with care."

"My word, Holmes!"

"Yes, Watson. There is an evil here that I have scarce encountered in my career."

"It does recall the Whitechapel murders, does it not?"

"In some respects, this crime and those are quite similar. What terrifies me is that I can discern a similar malevolence here as when I looked into those murders."

"What's to be done?"

"The police are still trying to ascertain the identity of the unfortunate woman. I fear though that is the least promising avenue of inquiry. While her past may shed some light upon her murder, I am more inclined to think that the symbols on her body offer a far more promising line of investigation."

"Do you have any idea what the images might signify?"

"If I were pressed, I should say they were druidic symbols."

"Why druidic?" I inquired.

"Because she was murdered on the vernal equinox, a day regarded as holy by both the ancient druids as well as their contemporary counterparts."

"My word," I exclaimed, "that certainly would give one pause. And are there modern druids?" I asked.

"Indeed," replied Holmes. "Right here in London, we have a chapter of the Ancient Order of Druids, a group that has been among us since the late 18th century."

"Ancient Irish priests in modern-day London! You can't be serious!" I exclaimed. "I thought that the Ancient Order of Druids was more a social club than a religious body."

"Well, that's what it appears to have evolved into over the decades since its founding, but we must consider the possibility of a coven of renegade members – perhaps entire lodges – discerning a certain wisdom in their pagan forbears and clamoring for a return to 'the old ways'."

"My word, Holmes!" I exclaimed. "You can't be serious."

"I have the mutilated body of a young woman crying for justice," said my friend. "I have never been more serious.

"These contemporary groups that exist in London were no doubt influenced – and inspired if you will – by two Welsh organizations, the Druid Society, which was based on Angelesey, or Ynys Môn, a small island off northwest coast of Wales; and the Society of the Druids of Cardigan, both of which were established sometime in the mid-18th century. I cannot vouch for the historical accuracy of either of those groups, but I can say with absolute certainty that their names and a portion of their iconography are based upon what was then believed about the ancient druids."

"And what exactly do we know of druids?" I ventured.

"Give me a moment," said Holmes, who then ventured into his bedroom and returned with a copy of Julius Caesar's "Gallic Wars" and another tome titled "The Origin of Tree Worship."

"You are just full of surprises, Holmes," I remarked. "'The 'Gallic Wars' and 'The Origin of Tree Worship.' I'll be damned."

"I believe you've seen the latter previously," said Holmes who then ignored me as he thumbed through the first book, "Ah, here it is," he remarked. "Allow me to paraphrase if you would:

"Throughout Gaul there are two classes of persons of definite account and dignity. One of these is the druids, and the other is the knights. The druids often concerned themselves with

7

questions with the worship practices and the due performances of sacrifices, both public and private, as well as the interpretation of ritual questions."

"Sacrifices," I exclaimed, "both public and private. Given your prologue, am I to conclude that their customs included human sacrifices?"

Holmes continued, "Caesar goes on to say that the druids offered human sacrifices, primarily for those who were gravely sick or in danger of death in battle. Huge wickerwork images were filled with living men and then burned; although the druids preferred to sacrifice criminals, they would choose innocent victims if necessary.

"I suspect, from what little I know of their religion at present and what Caesar tells us, that human sacrifices were a minor aspect of their belief system, and perhaps not even a core tenant."

"There was no wicker man at Stonehenge, was there?"

"No," my friend replied, "which makes me think that if this is a druidic sacrifice, it is, at best, tangentially related to their religious beliefs. No, Watson, I believe this is something else entirely, but for the life of me, I'd be hard-pressed to tell you what it is."

After a long pause, he added, "You have to realize, old friend, that the ancient Celts looked upon death as merely a passing of sorts. As I understand it, some druids believed in reincarnation and that the soul would be reborn in this world – perhaps as another person, perhaps as a rock or a tree."

"What utter poppycock!"

Holding up his copy of "The Origin of Tree Worship," Holmes remarked, "I'm not certain we should dismiss anyone's belief system that simply. After all, consider the basis of Christianity. They believe that their god assumed the guise of a man, lived among us and then was crucified so that the gates of heaven might be opened to man once again. I've found it's always best never to reject something out of hand just because we neither understand nor agree with it."

I found it hard to argue with my friend's sentiment on that particular point, so I opted to remain silent.

"I think it is imperative as we move forward that we keep an open mind. After all, as a medical man, you know that germs and bacteria, invisible to the naked eye, are responsible for infections and various diseases. You cannot see those organisms, yet you know that they exist."

"But that is a matter of science," I argued.

"Indeed," replied my friend, but arriving at your science must have required a giant leap of faith on someone's part in the past."

Knowing that to debate the point was fruitless, I simply said, "Agreed." I was more than happy to concede a small victory to my friend after the day he must have endured.

"What is your next move?" I asked.

"They are bringing the woman's body to London. In fact, it may have already arrived. I was hoping that you might accompany me to the morgue tomorrow and examine it with a practiced eye. I am afraid that I may have missed something amid all the hubbub at Stonehenge."

"I'd be happy to lend you whatever assistance I can."

"Splendid," said Holmes. "And now, perhaps a pipe before bed while you fill me in on your day?"

As I recounted the details of my rather mundane day, I could see that Holmes was only half listening. I knew his mind was miles away on the plains north of Salisbury, trying to make sense of what appeared to be on the surface a totally senseless and savage murder.

Chapter 2

The next morning, I awoke at nine and when I entered the sitting room, I found Holmes exactly where I expected him to be, sitting in his chair, poring over the morning papers.

"For a change, they seem to have all the facts correct, and as I suspected, there is nothing in the different reports of which I wasn't already aware."

Throwing the papers to the floor, Holmes stepped to the door and bellowed, "Mrs. Hudson, we are ready for breakfast."

A few minutes later, our landlady entered carrying a tray that bore two covered plates. "There's no need to yell, Mr. Holmes. I'm only downstairs. You could just ring the bell, you know."

"I do apologize, Mrs. Hudson, but I have a great deal on my mind, and I fear that you and Watson will bear the brunt of my frustration until I can make some headway with this case."

"No need to apologize, Holmes. We understand the situation and stand ready to assist you in any way we can, don't we, Mrs. Hudson?"

Looking at me and then Holmes, she nodded, saying, "The doctor speaks for both of us, Mr. Holmes."

After a rather awkward pause, Holmes looked at her and said, "I presume you have made toast as well?"

As she left, Holmes looked at me and muttered simply, "Thank you, Watson."

After we had finished our breakfast, we hailed a hansom cab and made our way to the Royal London Hospital, a place with which Holmes and I were all too familiar. We had visited the institution on Whitechapel Road a decade earlier, when the Ripper roamed free, terrorizing the inhabitants of the institution's environs.

As we entered the mortuary, I saw that Lestrade had already arrived and was deep in conversation with a veritable mountain of a man.

Turning to us, he said, "So you are here at last. Mr. Holmes and Dr. Watson, allow me to introduce Dr. Jeffrey Brewitt."

Although I've remarked upon my friend's height many times, Dr. Brewitt towered over Holmes, standing at least six inches taller than Holmes. After they had shaken hands, I stepped forward and said, "It is a great honor to meet you Dr. Brewitt. I found your article on proper post-mortems in the Lancet fascinating."

"We do what we can to spread light in a benighted world," said Brewitt amiably. "But enough of that; you gentlemen came here to learn about this girl." He led us to the table and pulled back the sheet to reveal the face of a woman in her early twenties. She had long fair hair and had likely been quite attractive when she was alive.

"Doctor Brewitt," said Holmes, "do you have any idea what the symbol on her forehead might mean?"

Looking past Holmes, I saw that three lines had been painted inside a circle on her forehead in what looked to be blood. They converged at the top, just below her hairline.

Here is a crude rendering.

"Actually, I do, Mr. Holmes. That symbol is called the 'awen.' It is an ancient druidic symbol that is used to represent inspiration. Generally, it refers to those individuals – poets, musicians and the like – who have been touched or inspired."

"I must say, doctor," said Holmes, "I am impressed by the breadth of your knowledge. From proper post-mortems to the symbols of ancient Celtic priests, are there any limits to your reservoirs?"

"There are many," replied Brewitt. "I know that symbol because my father was Irish and taught folklore, mythology and medieval literature at Trinity College. He was a bit disappointed that I didn't follow in his footsteps."

"I can only say that etymology's loss was physiology's gain," said Holmes.

"You flatter me, Mr. Holmes. Unfortunately, that is the only symbol on which I can shed any light. The others are unknown to me."

"And the cause of death? Have you been able to ascertain that?"

"She bled to death as the result of a very precise stab wound to her heart," replied Brewitt. "The weapon may have been a very sharp knife or perhaps even a scalpel. Given that it punctured the heart, I would say that death was nearly instantaneous, perhaps a moment or two at the most."

"Well, at least she didn't suffer terribly," said Lestrade.

"Do we know who she is?" asked Holmes.

"Not yet," replied Lestrade, "but we are working on it. You may rest assured."

Turning back to Brewitt, Holmes said, "I hope you will not take it amiss if I ask you to allow Dr. Watson to examine the body."

"Not at all, Mr. Holmes. I am as familiar with the doctor's literary efforts as he is with mine."

Donning a pair of gloves and an apron, I pulled back the sheet and saw that other symbols had been painted on the right side of the woman's abdomen, again in what I presumed to be her own blood.

At the time, I had no idea what they meant, but I have tried to reproduce them faithfully in the event that a reader might recognize them.

)‖Ⅴ‖‖Ⅰ(

Holmes looked at me inquiringly. "They look vaguely familiar," I said, "though, for the life of me, I cannot recall where I have seen them."

Holmes pulled a notebook from his pocket and reproduced the drawing as I have done here. When he had finished, he looked at us and said simply, "I feel a visit to the library at the British Museum is in order. You may continue here with Dr. Brewitt, and I shall meet you for dinner at Baker Street." Then he shook hands with Lestrade and Dr. Brewitt and strode out of the room.

"Well, that was a rather abrupt departure," remarked Brewitt.

"You must forgive Mr. Holmes," said Lestrade. "He's a bit like a bulldog when he is working on a case. Once he is on the scent, as he appears to be now, nothing else seems to matter.

"I'll be heading back to the Yard," continued Lestrade.

"If you should discover anything, I should like to know it before Mr. Holmes," said Lestrade, gazing at me pointedly. He concluded, "After all, I am the official detective assigned to this case."

Left to our own devices, Dr. Brewitt and I continued our examination of the body, which eventually yielded one surprising fact and one truly startling one.

Chapter 3

When I returned to Baker Street later that afternoon, I found Holmes curled up in his chair, pipe ablaze, with his fingers steepled under his chin.

"So, have you had a productive afternoon?" I asked.

"Indeed," replied Holmes. "I spent much of it with a Dr. Steven Smith, an expert on Anglo-Irish literature and history."

"Judging from the fact that you are sitting here thinking, I would have to conclude that Dr. Smith was able to shed some light on the mysterious symbols on the young woman's abdomen."

"Indeed," replied Holmes. "Have you ever heard of ogham?"

"No," I replied. "What is it?"

"According to Dr. Smith, the ancient Celts, more specifically the druids, devised an alphabet of some 20 characters. The letters themselves are fairly simple, being composed of vertical, horizontal and diagonal lines in various combinations. Each letter is associated with a particular tree, and as a result, each carries an array of connotations that add layers of meaning to its usage."

"That might explain the yew tree branches that were placed around the body," I said.

"To a degree," replied Holmes. "There are many ways to interpret the yew. One of which, oddly enough, is its signification of mystery."

"And are the letters on the girl ogham symbols?"

"If you believe Dr. Smith, and I see no reason to doubt his veracity, they are."

"Was Dr. Smith able to decipher their meaning?"

"Yes," replied Holmes. "After consulting one of his reference books, he was able to translate them quite easily."

"And what is their meaning?"

Holmes looked at me and pursing his lips, he said quietly, "Death."

"What does it all mean, Holmes? A dead girl marked with a druidic symbol and the letters of an obscure ancient Irish alphabet? And her body surrounded by yew branches?"

"I cannot even essay an answer, Watson. We need more data. Who was the girl? Why create the appearance of a sacrifice? Where do the Gaelic symbols lead us? Unfortunately, we have far more questions than we have facts. You know my methods, Watson. We cannot even begin to theorize until we know a great deal more. Tell me, did your afternoon with Dr. Brewitt bear any fruit?"

"I believe that it did."

Holmes looked at me expectantly as I paused to refill my pipe. "Get on with it, Watson!"

"On the back of her neck, hidden by her hair, we discovered a small puncture mark."

"Have you any idea what caused the wound?"

"I wouldn't call it a wound, Holmes. Brewitt and I both agree that it was made by a hypodermic. It is quite possible the girl was drugged before she was slain."

"I must admit that does strike me as rather odd," said Holmes. "A compassionate killer? Have you anything else to report?"

"Yes, although the girl appeared to be a blonde, her hair had been dyed very recently. When we discovered the puncture wound, we could just see the beginning of her own color – a deep brown – starting to grow in. Also, whoever removed her organs would appear to have some knowledge of anatomy. The cuts were clean and precise ..."

Holmes finished my sentence for me, "as though they had been made with a scalpel?"

I nodded in agreement.

"My, my," said Holmes, "To quote our old friend Mr. Dodgson, 'Curiouser and curiouser'."

"What do you make of it, Holmes?"

"I must know a great deal more before I could even attempt to answer that question, Watson. What we have at the moment is a collection of odd facts. It remains to be seen exactly how they fit together."

To say I was disappointed in my friend's response would be something of an understatement. I desperately wanted him to do something, but he seemed content to sit in his chair and smoke his pipe. Perhaps he was mulling over the various aspects, trying to assemble them in a rational whole. After a long silence, I bid him good night and headed off to bed.

The next morning, I found that Holmes had already departed. After breakfasting alone, I caught up on my correspondence. Around noon, I heard my friend ascending the stairs.

As he entered, I said, "You were up early."

"Yes, Lestrade sent a messenger to the house at seven o'clock to say that the dead girl had been positively identified."

"Well, that should help with your investigation," I said.

"I'm afraid not," he replied. "It appears that her name was Annie Lock, and that she had run away from a Scottish orphanage. It also seems that she and another young woman were planning to set sail for Canada. As you know, the economic situation has forced thousands of young people to emigrate from Scotland to Canada in hopes of a better life. From what I know, once there, the young people are viewed as little more than a cheap source of farm labor and domestic help."

"Still," I cried, "such a life is better than what befell her here."

"Yes," said my friend. "In both Scotland and Canada, she might have been cruelly used, but she certainly didn't deserve the fate she suffered at Stonehenge."

"Why do you say it 'appears' her name was Annie Lock?"

"Consider," said Holmes, "she had dyed her hair, perhaps in an effort to avoid detection. It seems only natural that she would change her name as well, does it not?"

I had no answer for my friend.

Over the next few weeks, with no new developments to claim the front pages of any of London's papers, the case slowly faded from the public's consciousness. I knew that Holmes had visited the various druidic societies in London and discovered that, for the most part, they were little more than well-meaning fraternal organizations. He summed up his efforts in those areas by saying, "There was nary a true pagan to be found."

As you might expect, Holmes was soon required to devote his attention to other, more pressing matters. I was glad to see my friend so busy, but I knew that in his free time, what little of it there was, he busied himself pursuing the few leads that came his way. Sadly, all of them, even the most promising, turned out to be dead ends. Trips to Salisbury to interview the girl's few acquaintances proved fruitless as well.

As the weather gradually warmed, we endured a rather wet April and a delightful May soon gave way to June. For at least six weeks, I had not heard Holmes, nor anyone else for that matter, utter the name of Annie Lock. In truth, I believe that she had slipped into the netherworld of half-forgotten memories. However, I soon learned that not everyone had dismissed the memory of the poor girl – at least not entirely.

It was near the end of the second week of June that I returned home one evening after a busy afternoon spent covering for a colleague. I entered our lodgings and discovered my friend kneeling on the floor, lens in hand, examining a large map that he had spread out in the middle of the sitting room and anchored with various reference volumes along the edges and corners.

He looked up as I entered. "Ah, Watson. I see Mrs. Eldridge has paid in kind again. I do hope this latest batch of preserves is better than her last."

"You see the bulge of the jelly jar in my coat pocket," I exclaimed.

"I might, if there were one to see," Holmes replied placidly.

Placing my hand in my empty pocket, I remembered that I had moved the jar from my pocket to my bag after I had been nearly knocked down on the street.

"Confound it, Holmes. How could you possibly know?"

He smiled and said simply, "Because I can see what you cannot."

"And what is it that I cannot see?" I asked, trying to contain myself.

"A daub of orange on your collar. I can only conclude that Mrs. Eldridge made you sample her effort, and that neither of you noticed that a small portion had soiled your shirt."

"Well," I laughed, "she has tried her hand at marmalade. As to whether it's an improvement, I shall let you ascertain that at breakfast tomorrow. In the meantime, what is this map and what are you studying?"

"I had Professor John Connors, the leading archaeological authority on the history of the British Isles, make this map for me."

"Never heard of him," I remarked.

"Perhaps you have heard of Augustus Pitt Rivers?"

"You mean General Pitt Rivers? What military man hasn't?"

"Well, General Pitt Rivers, who authored 'On the improvement of the rifle as a weapon for general use,' followed his inclinations after leaving the army and became an archaeologist of no small repute. That same General Pitt Rivers has served as a mentor to John Connors, so we are drawing upon the top experts in the field."

"But to what end, exactly? What is that a map of? And what field?"

"As you know, Stonehenge is not the only stone circle in Great Britain. In fact, according to Professor Connors, there are more than 1,000 such structures and they can be found in England,

Scotland, Ireland and Wales as well as the Channel Islands and Brittany."

"But why do you need such a map?"

"The summer solstice is but ten days away. Although I pray that I am wrong..."

"You anticipate another murder?"

"Yes, Watson. I do not think that Annie Lock's death was an isolated incident. If indeed, there is a cult of some sort at work here, I am hoping to prevent any future ... sacrifices."

Holmes uttered the last word with an obvious distaste for the significance it carried.

"And how do you plan to do that? The police cannot stake out more than 1,000 stone circles for an entire night in hopes of catching the perpetrators."

"Obviously. That is why I am trying to ascertain the most likely spots where such an incident might occur."

"And have you made any progress?"

"That remains to be seen," replied Holmes. "I am ill-suited for this type of work as I am merely grasping at straws. I am making nothing more than educated guesses, and I believe you know all too well how I feel about guessing.

"At any rate, if our killer wishes to remain close to London, I should think the Rollright Stones located between Oxfordshire and Warwickshire, on the edge of the Cotswold Hills, might offer some appeal. According to Professor Connors, there are three different sites, each dating from a different period.

"The oldest, the Whispering Knights dolmen, is believed to be from some 10,000 years ago."

"Dolmen?" I inquired.

"I apologize, Watson. It's just that I have become so steeped in these things that they are becoming second-nature to me. A dolmen is an above-ground tomb, made up of at least two vertical megaliths, or large stones, supporting a capstone, which acts as a sort of roof. The Rollright Stones are made up of the Whispering Knights dolmen; the King's Men, a stone circle with more than 70 members; and the King Stone, a single monolith."

"And what has this to do with druids?"

"Professor Connors informs me that similar circles can be found further north in the Lake District, including the Castlerigg Stone Circle. But I digress. Although the Rollright Stones is certainly one possibility, the stone circle at Avebury is less than 30 miles from Stonehenge. If I can persuade Lestrade to cover those two monuments – although I'm certain he is going to want to return to Stonehenge – you and I can travel north to keep watch on the Nine Ladies on Stanton Moor in Derbyshire. The Ladies were among the 28 archetypal monuments in England and Wales included in General Pitt-Rivers' Schedule to the first Ancient Monuments Protection Act, which became law in 1882. It was taken into state care the following year."

"My word, Holmes! You have been busy."

"Watson, there is an evil afoot, the likes of which I have seen only once before. We must do whatever is necessary to foil whatever plans it may be hatching, and if that includes a night on Stanton Moor, so be it."

And there again, I was privy to a glimpse behind the mask of indifference that my friend so often displayed to the world. I saw a man driven by a quest to right an unspeakable wrong. He was determined to catch the fiend who had killed Annie Lock before he or she could kill again. While the chase was important and his ego was involved, I knew that Holmes was spurred on more by a profound sense of justice than by any possibility of self-aggrandizement.

Over the next few days, I saw little of Holmes, and I assumed that he was making arrangements with Lestrade to have the various stone circles kept under observation on the night of the summer solstice.

The longest day of the year fell on a Wednesday, and the Monday before our trip, Holmes said to me "I want to leave as soon as possible tomorrow morning. I have found a small inn in Beeley, less than three miles from the circle. We will arrive as early as possible, lunch and then nap. Although it may be the shortest night of the year, I expect that we will find the waiting tedious and minutes turning to hours."

"I'll be ready, Holmes."

"And one more thing, Watson. Do bring your service revolver. I don't know what to expect, so I should like to be prepared for the worst."

Chapter 4

We departed from St. Pancras at approximately 8 a.m. Tuesday. By noon, we had reached the village of Matlock where we procured the services of a carriage to take us to Beeley. After a light lunch at the inn, we both retired to our rooms. The heat was oppressive, and I soon fell into a sound asleep. I was awakened by a gentle rapping on my door.

"Come in," I said.

"I hope you are well rested, Watson. I fear that we have a long night ahead of us."

After dining, we sat outside the inn, enjoying the cooler air as the sun slowly sank in the west. Tossing his cigarette aside, Holmes said, "I think we should set out for the Nine Ladies."

"Do you know where to go?"

"Yes. Professor Connors has drawn me quite a detailed map. I think when we get there, I shall conceal myself on the west side of the circle while you may take up a position on the east side, directly opposite.

"Connors has indicated that there is a gap at the south portion of the circle. From our concealments, we should be able to spot anyone approaching the circle, and if we are nimble enough, we should be able to apprehend them. However, I do want to get a look at the terrain in daylight, just in case there is anything Connors has omitted from his map."

Anyone who visits the Nine Ladies, expecting something on the order of Stonehenge, is doomed to disappointment. The Nine Ladies form a rather small circle, which measures approximately 40 by 35 feet.

Holmes and I arrived at the circle just as the last rays of light were visible in the west.

"There's really not much to see, is there?" I asked.

"No," replied Holmes, "The Nine Ladies are far less imposing than their counterparts in other sections of the country."

"Then why bring us here? What is it about this place that makes you think our killer will visit here?"

"As I explained, General Pitt-Rivers saw this as an important archaeological site. In fact, the circle is now under the care of the government, thanks to his efforts." Pointing south, Holmes asked, "Can you see that single stone over there?"

"Yes," I said, "just barely though."

"That is called the King Stone, just like at Rollright. If you believe the legend, the Nine Ladies were turned to stone for dancing on a Sunday. A bit fanciful for my taste," he said drily. "However, from my investigations, I have learned that the Ladies are quite popular among today's pagans.

"For those two reasons alone, I believe that the killer – if he does strike tonight – is far more likely to be found here than at Stonehenge."

We were now in near darkness, and Holmes said, "Let us take our places. You will hide behind that large rock over there while I will conceal myself here. Since we have no idea what to expect, I pray you wait for my signal before moving. Try to refrain from smoking, and whatever you do, please remain alert."

As I started to move away, Holmes thrust a small parcel in my hands and said, "This may help you stay awake."

When I had taken my position behind the stone, I opened the box and discovered a ham sandwich and a flask filled with hot tea. As you might expect, I was touched by my friend's kindness as well as his foresight.

To say that the night dragged on inexorably would not even begin to do justice to the ordeal. My only comfort was that Holmes was nearby and suffering much as I was. The hours passed slowly, and I must admit that I may have dozed off for a few minutes on more than one occasion. Suddenly, I heard voices and in the distance, I could see a lantern approaching the Nine Ladies. Although I had no idea what time it might be, I guessed that sunrise was not too far off.

Moving carefully so as not to make any noise, I peered around the stone that concealed me and thought I saw the outlines of three figures in the center of the circle. I had absolutely no idea what they were doing, until one of them struck a match to light a candle. Soon, all three of them were holding candles, and the lantern had been extinguished. As one of them reached into a sack, I heard Holmes exclaim, "Now, Watson."

Moving with all the speed I could muster, I headed for the gap in the circle, through which they had entered, in order to cut off their retreat. I thought I saw Holmes – although I might have just as easily imagined it – charging from his hiding place and grabbing one of the figures.

As you might expect, they had extinguished their candles as soon as they heard Holmes yell, and there were various voices hollering in the darkness. I didn't see anyone pass by me although I must admit that I really didn't see much of anything.

From across the circle, I heard my friend say, "Watson, are you hurt?"

"No, I'm fine Holmes. How about you?"

Suddenly, perhaps 20 feet in front of me, I saw the glow of a candle and a hooded figure, struggling in Holmes' grip.

Advancing, I said, "What have we here?"

Holmes pulled back the hood to reveal the face of a young woman who couldn't have been more than 16.

"Who are you? And what are you doing here?" Holmes demanded.

"Who are you?" replied the girl, "And what right do you have to restrain me?"

"My name is Sherlock Holmes," replied my friend.

As you might expect the transformation on the face of the young woman was immediate. "I know why you're here," she said, "because of the killing at Stonehenge a few months back."

"Yes," replied Holmes.

"We had nothing to do with that. Although we are the descendants of druids, we are here only to offer the fruits of our harvest to our gods, and you have no right to stop us."

"Actually, I do," replied Holmes. "This land belongs to the Crown, and Dr. Watson and I are assisting Scotland Yard in an investigation. So, unless, you would like to pay a visit to London and answer to Inspector Lestrade, perhaps the most fearsome policeman working today, I suggest you cooperate."

Turning to me she said, "I presume you are Dr. Watson." After I had nodded, she continued, "I have read your accounts of this Inspector Lestrade, he sounds barely competent, let alone fearsome."

Despite the semi-darkness, I could swear that I saw a smile flash across Holmes' face. He said to the woman, "What is your name and where are you from?"

"My name is Agnes, and I'm from Chesterfield."

"And what is in the sack?" asked Holmes.

"Fruits and vegetables for our offering," she replied. Handing the bag to Holmes, she said, "Here, see for yourself."

After Holmes had dumped its contents on the ground, I could see apples, ears of corn, some medium-sized gourds and various other types of produce.

"Agnes, may I give you some advice? What you believe and to whom or what your pray is entirely up to you, However, I think I should refrain from such overt acts of worship, especially on the solstices and the equinoxes, until this Stonehenge business has been resolved. Dr. Watson and I are not policemen, but I do think members of the official force might frown upon your actions. After all, even though you are a minor, tolerance has never been one of the law's strengths."

"You mean I'm free to go?"

"Yes, and take your offerings with you. I should advise you to counsel your friends as I have you. Trust me when I say, the fewer people that know of this, the better. Once the Stonehenge murder has been solved, you may dance under maypoles and do any number of other things to your heart's desire, but until then…," Holmes let the words trail off.

"I understand, Mr. Holmes and thank you very much." With that she gathered up her fruits and vegetables and walked off toward the south.

It suddenly occurred to me that the first traces of the sun were visible. I looked at Holmes and said, "That was quite a night, and what a magnanimous gesture on your part."

"Not at all," Holmes replied. "She did nothing wrong. Religion is a matter of personal choice and conscience. I may not approve of her choices but I will do nothing to impinge on her freedom."

As we walked back to the inn, I said, "Do you think the killer struck someplace else last night?"

"I should be very surprised if another murder did not occur, but I fear we must wait until we return to London to learn the details."

Little did I know how accurate my friend's prediction would prove to be.

Chapter 5

We passed the ride back to London in virtual silence. I could see that Holmes was deep in thought, and I knew from of our years of friendship that he disliked being disturbed when he was wrestling with a problem.

As we disembarked from our carriage, a young constable ran up to us. "Mr. Holmes, Inspector Lestrade ordered me to wait on this platform until you arrived. There has been another killing, sir."

"Where this time?" asked Holmes.

"In Uffington," replied the constable.

"The White Horse?" inquired Holmes.

"I do not know, sir. I was ordered to meet your train and escort you to Paddington where a special is being held to take you and Dr. Watson north to Uffington."

Within the hour, Holmes and I were once again heading north in a private car. About three hours later, we arrived in Farington and were once again met on the platform by a member of the police, only this time it was Lestrade himself.

After greetings had been exchanged, Lestrade said, "I have a carriage waiting."

During the ride, Holmes began to question Lestrade, asking, "Exactly what happened, Inspector?"

"Are you familiar with the White Horse of Uffington?" asked Lestrade.

"Although I have never seen it, I have heard of it. And I must confess that since the Stonehenge killing, I have learned somewhat more about it," replied Holmes.

"The body of a young man from Farington was found in the eye of the horse," said Lestrade. "Like the girl at Stonehenge, several of his organs had been removed and placed around the body. His face and abdomen were marked with strange symbols that appear to have been painted with his own blood, and placed around the body were branches that had been cut from a willow tree."

"So our killer has struck again," said Holmes, "but why here?"

"If we knew the answer to that, Mr. Holmes, I should think we might have him in custody by now," replied Lestrade.

"Am I likely to find any clues, or have the locals been trampling all over the crime scene?" asked Holmes.

"I'm afraid it's quite the latter," replied Lestrade. "I know your methods, Mr. Holmes, but by the time I was notified and made my way here from Avebury, I think every villager within ten miles must have stopped by to see what had happened."

"And you interviewed them, of course?" inquired Holmes.

"We did, sir, and quite thoroughly I might add," said Lestrade.

"So have there been any strangers in the vicinity recently?" asked Holmes.

"According to the different constables with whom I spoke, there have been a few visitors of late, but no one registered with any of the villagers. Unless, of course, you count the geologist who was here examining the horse a few weeks ago," said Lestrade.

"Hold that thought, Inspector."

With that my friend lapsed into silence.

Lestrade turned to me, "Is he doing that deducing thing again?"

"I'm certain that he is mulling over the crimes and looking for connections, but thus far he has been given precious little to work with." Lestrade and I continued to talk about the murders until we had reached Uffington Castle. As we drove past the castle and into the Vale of the White Horse, Holmes suddenly roused himself.

"Are we nearing Dragon Hill?" he inquired.

"Indeed, we are," replied Lestrade.

"Before we start the ascent, please ask the driver to stop."

A few minutes later the carriage came to a halt. We stepped down, and I must say that the view of the surrounding countryside was breathtaking. However, I saw that Holmes had his attention focused entirely on the famed White Horse.

Gazing across the valley, I saw the stark outline of the White Horse. I was struck by the primitive imagery and the power that it could still convey despite the passage of several millennia. I found out later that the outline is 300 feet long and approximately 130 feet high.

"Professor Connors tells me that outline is probably several thousand years old," remarked Holmes.

"You don't say," remarked Lestrade, with obvious disinterest. "And that is important because?" he continued.

"We are once again at one of Britain's mysterious landmarks, trying to solve a murder," said Holmes. "I should think the connection would be obvious, even to you."

"I can see the obvious, Mr. Holmes," replied Lestrade. "I just don't understand it."

"Neither do I – yet. However, the White Horse has been there for centuries. Like Stonehenge, it is now under the protection of the state," continued Holmes. "There is a history here, just as there is at Stonehenge. Did you know that for centuries, villagers would come out every few years to remove vegetation from around the various sections and to scour the horse and add new chalk to keep the outline clear and distinct?"

"I'll tell you what's clear, Mr. Holmes. The body of a young man was found stabbed to death and mutilated, just like the girl at Stonehenge. This cannot go on."

"I quite agree, Lestrade. Let us examine the scene."

We drove to the top of the White Horse Hill, remaining a respectful distance from the carving. Off to the right, I could see a group of officers conversing and on the ground, I could see a sheet, covering what I presumed was the body.

It had been left in the middle of a white chalk circle that served as the horse's eye. The circle was contained in a larger square-like shape that represented the horse's head. After we made our way to it, Holmes pulled back the sheet halfway, revealing the rather handsome face of a young man who appeared to be about eighteen with tousled blond hair. He was shirtless, and I presumed naked. On his forehead a symbol had been painted in blood. As I bent closer, I could see that there was again a single stab wound below the heart. I remember thinking that whoever our killer was, he or she had had some experience with a knife.

Trying to appear inconspicuous, I looked for and spotted a slight puncture mark on his neck. Surrounding the body were three willow branches, which Holmes later informed me, were arranged exactly as the yew branches had been placed around the body at Stonehenge.

After I finished my examination, I pointed to the boy's forehead and said, "Why that looks like the horse itself."

"I believe you are right, Watson."

"What does it mean?" asked Lestrade.

"Hold on a minute," said Holmes.

Lowering the sheet, he revealed a second symbol that had been painted on the left side of the man's abdomen.

"Have you any idea what the symbols mean?" I asked.

"I do not," replied my friend with a quiet determination, "but I intend to find out."

Holmes said to Lestrade, "I would like the body taken to Dr. Brewitt. Watson, I should like you to accompany the boy and see if Brewitt can tell us what the symbol on the boy's forehead means."

"What will you be doing?" I asked.

"Talking to the villagers," replied Holmes, "on the off chance that Lestrade and his men may have missed something."

I didn't dare turn around because I didn't want to see the anger on Lestrade's face. To my surprise, he remained silent, and then the realization washed over me: The only way that Holmes was going to bring the killer to heel was if Lestrade cooperated, and I think Lestrade had arrived at the same conclusion.

Chapter 6

I followed Holmes' instructions to the letter. We transported the body to London by train, and then a police wagon carried the corpse to the Royal London Hospital.

As Lestrade hovered over us, Brewitt and I conducted a thorough post-mortem. "He died from the stab wound just below the heart. Once again, the knife punctured the organ causing the heart to cease beating," Brewitt remarked. Looking at his face, I could see that he had spotted the puncture mark and was about to remark on it when I surreptitiously raised a finger to my lips, but he had begun before he noticed my warning.

"And...," Brewitt started.

"And what?" inquired Lestrade.

"And the wound must have been inflicted by a man of some strength," he added.

Brewitt then nodded at me, and I continued, "Mr. Holmes would like to know if you can tell us anything about the horse symbol on the boy's forehead."

"In druidic lore, the horse is often associated with the goddess, Epona," Brewitt remarked. "She is generally regarded as a goddess of fertility, and you will find her mentioned by the Roman satirist Juvenal as well as in 'The Golden Ass' by Apuleius. She has associations with similar goddesses in other cultures. If my father were still alive, I am certain that he would be able to tell you a great deal more, Dr. Watson."

After we had concluded the post-mortem, I returned to Baker Street. I expected to find the rooms empty, and I was not disappointed. I suspected that Holmes had spent the night near Uffington, talking to people and looking for clues.

When he arrived home early the next evening, I could tell immediately that his quest had been a fruitless one.

After he had gotten settled and filled his pipe, he began, "I believe I have remarked in the past how the countryside terrifies me. Where you see Nature in all her finery, I see only isolated areas and am struck by the impunity with which crimes may be committed there."

"No one will ever accuse you of being a romantic," I observed.

"I prefer to think of myself as a pragmatic realist," he countered. "I believe that I have told you that it is my contention that the lowest and vilest alleys in London do not present a more dreadful record of sin than does the smiling and beautiful countryside."

"Am I to take it then then that your investigation yielded nothing of substance?"

"The locals had trampled the scene so badly that there were literally scores of footprints. No, our killer is extremely careful," observed Holmes. "Although his cunning certainly makes him difficult to catch, it also allows me to weed out any number of individuals that the police might consider suspects.

"By the way," he continued, "how was your day at the Natural History Museum?'

"How on earth could you know where I have been?" I asked. "Are you having me followed?"

"Watson, I assure you that I have just returned to London within the hour and spoken to no one except yourself. As to your whereabouts today, I should think it rather obvious."

"Not to me," I said.

"Has it been raining all day?" asked Holmes.

"No, it was clear in the morning. The rain didn't start until the afternoon."

"Yet, your shoes are still bright and shiny. Your coat and hat are but slightly damp, as I noticed when I was hanging mine up. Taken together, those two facts indicate to me that you spent the majority of the day, or at least the afternoon, indoors."

"I will grant you that," I said, "but how do you know I wasn't at my club all afternoon?"

"Today is Thursday. You never go to your club on this day because you know that Colonel Walker is there, and you have repeatedly told me how tired you are of listening to his war stories. Moreover, you are using a new tobacco that you just purchased."

"True enough. I avoided my club and did stop at my tobacconist, but how did you determine that I had spent the day at the museum?"

"That was the easiest part of all," remarked Holmes.

"But how did you arrive at the Natural History Museum? Why not the Science Museum or the Victoria and Albert Museum?"

"Because ever since you stopped going to James J. Fox, you've been saving a few shillings by buying from Becton's on Thurloe Street. I can only conclude that after making your purchase and exiting Becton's, you found yourself threatened by

39

showers. With no umbrella for protection, you headed for the closest shelter, the Natural History Museum."

"Bravo, Holmes. But I must tell you, had I taken just a few more steps along Cromwell Road, I might have had the last laugh."

"True. Sometimes I do put too fine a point on it, but then you know my flair for the dramatic."

"All too well," I laughed. "So what did you learn in Uffington?"

"The boy was named Jeremy Mason. He was 18 and working as an apprentice to the local butcher. I spoke with his parents and what few friends he had and learned next to nothing."

"So we are stymied once again?"

"For the moment," he said, as he refilled his pipe. After drawing deeply, he began, "Let us consider what we know. Two young people were murdered, one on the vernal equinox and the other on the summer solstice. Their bodies were found on two prehistoric site separated by approximately 40 miles. Both were discovered nude, with various organs having been removed and placed about the bodies; both bore a druidic mark on their forehead and ogham writing on their torso, and both bodies were surrounded by branches cut from different types of trees. The obvious implication to be drawn is that our victims were in some way sacrificed at the behest of a druidic cult.

"Have I summed it up neatly enough?"

"Indeed," I replied, "but don't forget that both may have been drugged before they were killed."

"Thank you, Watson. Of all the aspects in this case, that is the one that I find the most baffling."

"And why is that?"

"Because people kill for any number of reasons – money, anger, jealousy, love, hatred – but seldom, if ever, do they take the time to make certain that their victims are spared the pain. No, Watson. It will not hold. There is something else at work here, but I must admit that at the present, I haven't the faintest idea what it is."

"So what's to be done?"

"I will continue my investigations," said Holmes, but I'm afraid that, to quote the poet, Milton, 'They also serve who only stand and wait'."

"You can't mean …"

"I'm afraid, I do, Watson. We must possess our souls in patience until the autumnal equinox."

"You must stop this madness, Holmes."

"Would that I could, my friend. Would that I could."

Chapter 7

As the summer dragged on, Holmes found himself involved with an array of "pretty little problems." There were several interesting cases, chief among them was the adventure that I have titled "The Case of the Meandering Marigolds." Unfortunately, none seemed to shed any light on the murders, and Holmes continued to spend much of his free time at the British Museum, running theories past Connors and attempting to cram the little attic of his mind with all types of information that I knew he would never have concerned himself with under other circumstances.

When he was not at the museum, he was trying to learn all that he could about the various druidic societies that had come so much into vogue. As a result, between excursions to the museum and nightly meetings of the various groups, many of which he attended in various disguises, his days were filled from dawn to dusk.

I have often remarked on my friend's tenaciousness, and this case was certainly no exception. His inability to make any real headway was consuming him, as had the contents of the hypodermic that he had once kept on the mantel.

In fact, I was so concerned with his behavior that I had decided to address him about it. I was dissuaded from it by the fact that one day in the middle of July, the 16th to be exact, Holmes returned home in what I can describe only as jubilant mood.

I was sorely tempted to ask my friend what had occasioned the change in his demeanor, but I knew that he would get around to it in his own good time.

After we had eaten, he suddenly broke the silence, "Watson, I must thank you for your forbearance with regard to this problem."

"Think nothing of it, old man," I replied.

"No, you have been the picture of patience, tolerating my comings and goings at odd hours and my moods of deep despair."

"Nothing new there," I said lightly.

Holmes smiled, looked at me, and said simply, "Good old Watson! I should be lost without you."

"What has occasioned this bit of introspection?"

"As I was talking with Professor Connors today, we were trying to ascertain where the killer might strike next. And suddenly, it hit me. We were doing our best to guess – and you know how I feel about guessing. We are working with precious few facts, none of which, I now know, can be used to illuminate the darkness of the future.

"I can do a great many things," said Holmes modestly. "However, even I cannot predict what is to come. I would like to be busy planning and baiting a trap of some sort, but it suddenly occurred to me that all my planning would be for naught. We anticipate a third killing, but we cannot be certain that there will be one.

"As a result, I must be as patient with the killer as you have been with me. I do think our murderer will strike again, but I have no idea where. While I am reasonably certain of the 'when,' but until that day draws near, my hands are tied."

"So you will do nothing?" I exclaimed.

"No, Watson. On the contrary, I will do everything in my power to catch this fiend, but I must have more information. I just hope that the unwary citizens are not asked to pay too high a cost."

"Perhaps, you have hit upon have something there," I remarked. "Thus far, there has been precious little publicity linking the two killings. Perhaps if we raised a hue and cry in the press, it would put people on their guard – at least around the time of the autumnal equinox."

"You make a splendid argument of the need for public awareness. Lestrade and I have gone back and forth over this. He is loath to publicize the killings, fearing the Yard will be embarrassed."

"Would those running the Yard like to have a few more murders on their hands?" I interjected, "so they can really be shown to be fools?"

"That is the point I will take up with the good Inspector on our next encounter, which should occur rather soon," said Holmes, glancing at his watch.

"How can you be so sure of that?"

"The Inspector and I have been meeting regularly. Sometimes, in his office at the Yard but more often than not in neutral locations – far from eavesdroppers. Earlier today, I sent him a message suggesting that we convene here tonight.

"In fact, he should be arriving any minute."

"Would you like me to leave?"

"Heavens, no," replied Holmes. "I know that I would welcome your observations, and I am equally certain that Lestrade would as well."

Before I could reply, I heard the bell ring, and after looking at his watch, Holmes remarked, "If nothing else, Lestrade is punctual."

A minute later the good Inspector entered the room,

"Good evening, Mr. Holmes, Dr. Watson," he said.

"Inspector," I countered.

"Sit down, Lestrade," Holmes said. "We have much to discuss. I hope you don't mind but I've asked Dr. Watson to join us tonight."

"Not at all," said Lestrade. Looking at me, he asked, "What do you make of this?"

"That's really not my bailiwick," I said, "but I do believe that you have a killer on your hands who poses a very real threat to public safety."

"I agree, Doctor, but you know how people are. Tell them you have a murderer on the loose, and they'll be looking for another Jack the Ripper hither and yon."

"But what's to be gained by concealing the truth?" I asked.

"The killer doesn't know we're onto him," answered Lestrade rather smugly. "He has no idea that we have connected the two killings."

I looked at Holmes beseechingly, and he said to Lestrade, "My dear Inspector, I am afraid I must side with the good doctor on this one. Thus far, at least, I am not onto anything. Have you made any progress with your lines of inquiry?"

"No," admitted Lestrade. "We have no leads and precious few clues. But I don't want to alarm the public needlessly."

"Needlessly," I spluttered. "Two people have been brutally murdered, and it may be just the beginning."

Lestrade grew red-faced, but before he could respond, Holmes said quietly, "I think I may have hit upon a compromise, Inspector."

After taking a moment to compose himself, Lestrade said, "And what would that be?"

"We have 69 days before the autumnal equinox on September 23rd. Suppose we keep everything out of the papers until the first of that month, and then if we have made no serious headway, we will inform the press that Scotland Yard has linked the two earlier murders and is pursuing several promising leads, but until the killer is captured, the public should be quite careful – especially in the days leading up to the equinox."

"While I don't like it," said Lestrade, "I can certainly see the merit in your position, Mr. Holmes."

"I think we would be remiss in our duty to the public if we failed to warn them," Holmes said.

"Yes," mused Lestrade, "and it is possible that the idea of several leads being vigorously pursued may give the killer pause."

Holmes and Lestrade then spent the better part of an hour rehashing what they knew and suggesting various avenues of investigation. Occasionally, I would interject something, but my contributions might best be termed miniscule.

It was only after Lestrade had departed that I said to my friend, "I just have one question, Holmes."

"Just one?"

"Do you really think that saying the Yard is following up on a number of promising leads will dissuade the killer?"

"Absolutely not, Watson. I am firmly convinced that –
barring a great stroke of luck – someone will die in a most
gruesome fashion on the morning of September 23rd."

Chapter 8

As July gave way to August and we began inching toward September, I knew that Holmes had made little, if any, progress on the case.

As I have said, he appeared to have come to terms with his own lack of momentum, which he attributed to "a lamentable absence of facts."

On the first of September, I was summoned at 3 a.m. to attend to a grievously ill patient in Pall Mall. After ministering to him, I returned to our lodgings, and as I stepped down from the cab, I could hear a newsboy hawking papers. He was lustily yelling, "Crazed killer on the loose. Read all about it."

Knowing that Holmes would have already obtained copies of all the pertinent broadsheets, I ascended the stairs to our rooms, where I was surprised to discover that he had already gone out.

Hungry and exhausted, I read all the papers as I enjoyed a full breakfast of scrambled eggs and a rasher of bacon. I was happy to see the story although it seemed to me that Lestrade had overplayed the Yard's role in linking the two cases while Holmes was not even mentioned.

I was wondering whether the omission had been at my friend's direction as I slowly nodded off in my chair.

Sometime later, I was gently roused from my slumber by Holmes, who had returned to our rooms without my hearing him.

"What time is it?"

"It is nearly two," he replied. "I can see that you have read the papers."

"I have indeed, and I should think Lestrade must be quite pleased with himself." Picking up the paper, I read aloud, "After painstaking research, Scotland Yard has concluded that there are certain common elements that would appear to tie together the murders of a young woman at Stonehenge last March and a young man at the White Horse of Uffington in June.

"My word, Holmes, a child could see that the two killings were almost identical. 'Painstaking research,' what absolute twaddle.

"While refusing to speculate or divulge any pertinent information about the killings, Inspector Lestrade would say only that there were obvious similarities that appeared to link the two murders and that the Yard was following up on several promising leads.

"He didn't tell them that the killings occurred on the solstice and the equinox?" I asked.

"He wanted to withhold that piece of information," Holmes said.

"But why? I thought the sole purpose of giving the press the story was to raise public awareness of the danger posed by the pending autumnal equinox."

"As did I," said Holmes. "It would seem that to a degree Lestrade has either reneged on our agreement or been told what he could make pubic."

"So what's to be done?"

"It has been taken care of," said Holmes.

"You don't mean…"

"The press have many sources," said Holmes with a sly grin, "some official – and some not. However, if the killer thinks the Yard a bunch of incompetents that may be to our advantage."

The next morning I awoke to discover that Holmes had once again risen early and left for a meeting with Dr. Connors.

However, on the table propped against a candlestick was a note that had been folded in two.

On the outside in Holmes' rather spidery writing were the initials "J.W."

On the inside was a short request;

"Watson,

After you have breakfasted, would you be so kind as to pick up an extra copy of today's papers? I believe that you will find the lead story of some interest.

SH"

After eating, I went downstairs and even before I had opened the door, I could hear the newsboy bellowing: "Yard seeks deadly druid! Public warned about seasonal killer!"

Chapter 9

"It would appear as though Scotland Yard has finally linked the two murders," he announced one afternoon.

"I should think they made the connection immediately after the second killing," she replied. "After all, they certainly had enough clues between the druidic symbols and the ogham writing."

"Yes, I agree, so why wait until now to make that information public?"

"I'm inclined to think they anticipated having the killers in custody by this point and then there would be no need to alarm the public unnecessarily."

"I suppose you are right," he replied.

"Have you made all the preparations for the next one?" she asked.

"I have."

"And the location that I selected is to your liking?" she asked.

"It does have a definite sense of drama, I will you give you that, acushla. But doesn't its relative newness rather undermine everything that we have done thus far?"

"Not at all," she replied. "After all, it is a re-creation of sorts, and I should think that with the other stone circles nearby, this will just add another element of confusion. Feel free to disagree, since you are the one doing the work, but in my opinion, it suits our needs perfectly," she said, a bit chafed at his lack of enthusiasm at her selection.

Suddenly it hit her, "You're not getting cold feet, are you?"

"Not if you are certain that this is the only way," he said.

"It was the only thing I could think of at the time," she replied. "And I think we have come too far to give up now. To quote the beloved Bard, 'I am in blood stepped in so far that should I wade no more, returning were as tedious as go o'er'."

"Macbeth, Act III, Scene 4," he replied. "Now there's someone who knew a bit about blood-letting. 'Gentle Will' indeed. 'Then I'll screw my courage to the sticking place'," he laughed.

"I'm impressed," she said.

"Don't be. There were several assignments while I was abroad where I had little else to do but read."

"So then we are in agreement?"

As he gazed at her face with its incredible beauty, he realized that he would do anything, no matter how heinous, so long as he could continue basking in the sunlight of her radiance.

"As always, my dear, I remain your humble servant to command."

Chapter 10

As the autumnal equinox drew near, the papers all carried stories warning the public about possible danger on the nights of September 22nd and possibly the 23rd. As a by-product of the stories, several meetings of the various druidic societies in London were disturbed by ruffians demanding to know if they were shielding a killer. In one instance, the secretary of a group was badly beaten as he tried to restore order, and several hooligans were arrested.

The city, and I suppose the entire country as well, was in an ugly mood. Holmes refrained from entering the fray, continuing to pursue his own line of inquiries and meeting frequently with Lestrade and Professor Connors.

Finally, on the morning of September 22nd, I asked my friend, "So where will we be keeping our vigil tonight?"

"Right here," he replied rather coolly.

"Here?" I asked incredulously.

"Indeed. You saw what happened when we traveled north in the summer. I lost an entire day before I could get to the crime scene. Who knows what clues were missed because I decided to lend the police a hand and keep watch on the Nine Ladies. No, Watson, I shan't make that mistake again.

"Lestrade has assigned teams to a number of historic sites. They have been in place for several days now, posing as laborers and farmhands, and they will be on hand at a number of locations tonight, including Arbor Low, which if I were a betting man, I would make the favorite."

"Arbow Low?"

"It's about 170 miles northwest of London. There, some 50 large limestone blocks form a rough oval, with monoliths at the entrances, and possibly a portal stone at the south entrance. There is also a large pit at the north entrance, which possibly contained a stone. In the center lie seven smaller blocks, forming a sort of cove. The stones are surrounded by an oval earthen bank. According to Professor Connors few henge monuments in the British Isles are as well preserved as this one.

"In addition to Arbor Low, there are men ensconced at towns and villages near Rollright, Avebury and Castlerigg."

"My word, Holmes. You certainly have been thorough."

"None of that is my doing," he replied. "Give the credit to Lestrade."

"Do I detect a note of cynicism in your voice?"

"Indeed, you do. As I told Lestrade, there are more than 1,000 such locations in England alone. Hundreds more if you add Ireland, Scotland, the Channel Islands and Normandy. The police simply do not have enough man-power to keep watch on all of them. With no idea of where the killer might strike next, I feel that my time is best spent here.

"Besides, Watson, I have set up a network of my own."

"What?" I exclaimed.

"Dr. Connors has been kind enough to provide me with a list containing all the names of the top historians and antiquarians scattered throughout the country. Should our killer strike, I expect to have an expert in place who can tell me more about the site as well as the goings-on in his own area."

"Bravo, Holmes. Does Lestrade know of your plans and your assistants?"

"Now that you mention it," my friend said, "I may have forgotten to mention it to the good Inspector.

"Please remind of my failing memory," he said with a wry smile, "at our next meeting with Lestrade.

"And now," said Holmes, "Mrs. Hudson has prepared an excellent dinner of stuffed, baked trout and afterwards, perhaps we can visit Mycroft at the Diogenes Club, and see what insights he may provide on these events."

Despite the impending sense of doom, we made short work of the trout. After that, we took a cab to Pall Mall, but Mycroft was not at the Diogenes Club.

"I can only think that the government has him working on something of grave importance," said Holmes after we had left that singular establishment.

Although the weather was unseasonably warm, the sky looked threatening. As a result, Holmes and I took a cab back to our lodgings, and it was only about 10 minutes later that the heavens opened. What had been a rather delightful late summer day ended with a squall and fierce rains heralding the arrival of autumn.

As we sat there, warm and dry, enjoying a nightcap and the last pipe of the day, I said to Holmes, "Perhaps the elements will deter our killer."

"Perhaps," he remarked. "Let us wait and see what news the morning brings."

When I awoke the next morning, I found Holmes enjoying his breakfast. "Why didn't you wake me?" I asked.

"I saw no reason. It's now nearly ten and there has been no word from Lestrade. I can only hope that, as you suggested, the rain dissuaded our killer."

I didn't think that Holmes was being entirely sincere, for I thought I detected a touch of sarcasm in his voice. Although I knew my friend was happy that the killer had not struck, I could also sense his disappointment in not having any leads to pursue in his investigation.

I went out later that morning as I needed to visit my tailor. Holmes declined to come with me, preferring to wait at Baker Street. After making my purchase, I lunched at my club. When I returned home around three in the afternoon, I found Holmes poring over a map of England.

"Still no word?" I asked.

"Not yet," he replied.

"Are you expecting to be summoned?"

"I am."

"What has changed your mind?"

"Murderers are often creatures of habit. Consider the similarities between the bodies. They were mutilated in an identical fashion and the marks on both were arranged in the same way, using the same symbols and that same ogham writing. No, Watson, the more I consider the problem, the more I am convinced that the weather does not matter to our killer. What concerns me more is the fact that he wants the bodies to be found. He craves the attention, though I could not begin to explain why.

"No, I am convinced that someone was murdered last night, but what I fear is that if the body is not discovered in a timely fashion, he may well kill again in a place where the body will be found."

As usual, Holmes was correct. Around five in the afternoon, we received a telegram from Lestrade. "This is what I was expecting," said Holmes, who then proceeded to read it aloud.

"Body found at Drizzlecombe on Dartmoor. Stop. Come at once. Stop. Have reserved a special train at Paddington. Stop. Awaiting your reply. Stop. Lestrade. Stop."

After he had finished, Holmes looked at me and said, "Come Watson. We have no time to lose."

Holmes then told the messenger to tell Lestrade that we would join him at Paddington as soon as possible.

As I went to pack my bag, Holmes said, "I have my stick. It couldn't hurt if you were to bring your revolver."

Some ten minutes later, I found myself in a cab with Holmes hurtling toward Paddington Station. When we arrived, we found Lestrade waiting for us. "This is a bad business that is getting worse," said the Inspector.

"It has been bad from the beginning," replied my friend. "Is there anything you can tell me?"

"The victim was, a young man, found late this morning near a tall stone at Drizzlecombe or Thruselcombe."

"Your telegram said Drizzlecombe," said Holmes impatiently. "Is there nothing else you can add?"

"He was discovered by a historian who was out checking the condition of the various historic sites."

"Have you identified the young man?"

"Not yet," replied Lestrade, "but the local authorities are working on it."

At that point, we boarded the train, and after we had settled in, Holmes asked, "Have you any idea how far this is from Lew Trenchard?"

I remember wondering what or who Lou Trenchard was and thinking to myself, "What an odd question," but I knew that Holmes had a reason for asking it.

"I believe that Lew Trenchard is approximately 20 miles away as the crow flies," said Lestrade. "From what I understand, the man who discovered the body first reported it to the owner of Lew Trenchard, the Reverend Sabine Baring-Gould. In fact, it appears to have been he who sent the telegram."

"Excellent," said Holmes.

"Why do you say that, Mr. Holmes?"

"The Rev. Sabine Baring-Gould is one of the leading antiquarians in all of Britain, and the top expert for the region of Dartmoor."

Holmes then shot me a knowing look, and I recalled his conversation of the previous evening about his assistants.

"I know that name," I said, "but not in connection with history."

"No," replied Holmes. "The Rev. Baring-Gould is a rather remarkable man. He authored 'The Book of Were-Wolves' as well as 'Curious Myths of the Middle Ages,' not to mention two novels, including 'The Broom Squire'."

"No," I said, "Although I have heard of the werewolf book, I know the name in connection with something else.

At that point, Holmes began to hum "Onward Christian Soldiers."

"That's it," I exclaimed.

"Yes," replied Holmes, "he also wrote the lyrics for the hymn and then Sir Arthur Sullivan composed the melody. While Baring-Gould had titled his work 'Hymn for Procession with Cross and Banners,' it was subsequently renamed 'St. Gertrude' after Sullivan had composed the music."

"So how on earth did it become 'Onward Christian Soldiers'?" I asked.

"The Salvation Army, apparently enamored of its militaristic theme, simply adopted it," replied Holmes.

"Author, composer, antiquarian, this Rev. Baring-Gould sounds quite the accomplished fellow," remarked Lestrade.

"Indeed, he is," replied Holmes. "He is also the current president of the Royal Institution of Cornwall. In that capacity he is involved with the Royal Cornwall Museum, which maintains a permanent display on the history of Cornwall from prehistoric times to the present day. Add to his many other accomplishments a book on Dartmoor, and I should think that we will be in excellent hands when we arrive at Drizzlecombe."

"I must say, Holmes, I am impressed," said Lestrade.

"You flatter me, Inspector," said my friend, barely concealing a smug grin.

We spent the rest of the journey, which took us nearly eight hours, discussing various aspects of the case.

As we pulled into the station at Plymouth, I asked the question that I knew had been on everyone's mind. "Holmes, the first two murders were relatively close to London, compared to this one. Why do you suppose our killer – if indeed it is the same person – has wandered so far afield?"

"That, Watson, is what terrifies me the most. As I said earlier, murderers are creatures of habit. On the surface, this does not appear to follow the pattern, except that it has taken place at another prehistoric site. No, I'm afraid we must wait to see the body, before we can say with absolute certainty whether we have just one killer to catch or two murderers to apprehend."

"You don't really think…," started Lestrade.

"I will say no more on the subject until I have seen the body," replied Holmes.

I looked at Lestrade, smiled in commiseration and did the only thing I could think to do, shrug my shoulders.

Chapter 11

Since we had arrived so late in the evening, we spent the night at a small inn in the village of Yelverton, and the next morning, we made our way to Drizzlecombe, hiking across the moor.

Located about four miles east of Yelverton, on the western side of the moor, Drizzlecombe can be found in a large open field. The primary attractions for historians and antiquarians are three stone rows, each of which is associated with a particular barrow and a very tall stone at the end, called a menhir.

There was a small group of men waiting for us at the closest stone row. They were standing fairly close to a stone column that I guessed to be about fifteen feet tall.

As we made our way across the field, one of the men left the group and met us about halfway. "I am Inspector Kenneth McKendry from the Devon Police." Turning to Lestrade, with whom he shook hands, he said, "It's good to see you again, Inspector."

Then he turned to Holmes and me and said, "And you must be Mr. Sherlock Holmes and Dr. Watson. I am so glad that you could join Inspector Lestrade. I'm afraid we're going to need all the help we can get on this one. It's not something that we see every day here."

"Have you identified the victim?" asked Holmes.

"We have, Mr. Holmes. He was the Honorable Trent Deveron, he was a 17-years-old, a baronet and a student at the Exeter School."

"Has the family been notified?" asked Holmes.

"Yes, sir," replied McKendry. "I dispatched a man to Tilverton last night after we learned his identity."

"How did you come by the information so quickly?" asked Holmes.

"Earlier in the day, we received a wire from William Buckley, the headmaster, informing us that one of his students, young Mr. Deveron, had gone missing. After we arrived, one of my men discovered a bag containing an Exeter blazer and the rest of the boy's clothing under a bush not too far from the body."

"Speaking of discoveries," said Lestrade, "who found the body?"

"I am getting a bit ahead of myself," apologized McKendry. "Please allow me to introduce you to the Rev. Sabine Baring-Gould and his associates, Robert Burnard and Richard Hansford Worth."

"Rev. Baring-Gould, I must say that it is an honor to meet you," said Holmes.

"The honor is mine, Mr. Holmes. Even out here on Dartmoor, we have heard of your exploits, and I never cease to marvel at your powers of deduction."

"I am afraid that those are somewhat exaggerated," said Holmes modestly.

"And you must be Dr. Watson," said Baring-Gould, shaking my hand warmly. "I must say that I have enjoyed your chronicling of Mr. Holmes' adventures."

"I am just sorry we had to meet under these circumstances," said Holmes, deftly steering the conversation back to the investigation. "Who was it that actually discovered the body?"

"Richard, did," said Baring-Gould, pointing to one of his associates.

"How did you happen to be in this remote place?" asked Holmes.

"Several years ago," Hansford Worth began, "Robert, Sabine and I re-erected this stone. We dug down several feet and poured concrete so that it would remain upright. Periodically, we examine the various sites on the moor that we have enumerated and catalogued, and as luck, would have it, I rode by 'The Bone' yesterday, and saw the body."

"The Bone?" asked Lestrade.

"That is the name the locals have given this particular stone," explained Baring-Gould, pointing to the column. "If you look at it from a certain angle, it's easy to understand why the appellation was bestowed and why it has stuck."

"May I examine the body?" asked Holmes, looking at Lestrade and McKendry.

"Please do, Mr. Holmes," said Lestrade.

I followed Holmes to the body, where he pulled back a sheet, revealing the face of a handsome young man with dirty blonde hair. On the boy's forehead was another symbol, presumably drawn in the young man's blood.

Looking at Baring-Gould and the others, Holmes asked, "Are any of you familiar with this symbol?"

"Of course," Baring-Gould replied, "that's the triquetra. You perhaps know it as the trinity knot. In a way, it resembles the ouroboros, does it not?" asked the reverend.

"Do you know what it means?" asked Holmes, trying to control himself.

"It is an ancient infinity symbol," explained the reverend. "You can see how the triquetra is actually one continuous line interweaving around itself, and as a result indicating the lack of a beginning or an end. Within that context, it is often regarded as symbol of eternal spiritual life."

"Does it relate to the druids in any way?" asked Holmes.

"I should say so," replied Baring-Gould. "Although my knowledge of Celtic mythology is rather limited. I do know that the Celts believed that everything important in the world was made up of threes. They believed in three stages of life, three basic elements, three domains; earth, sea and sky; past, present and future; mind, body and soul.

"It is one of the oldest symbols in Celtic mythology, and you can see its descendant in the shamrock, so beloved of the Irish."

"Would that correlate in some way with the three hazel branches that have been arranged around the body?" asked Holmes

Before Baring-Gould could answer, Lestrade, unable to contain himself any longer, interjected, "That's a symbol of eternal life, you say? Well, it certainly didn't do this lad much good, did it?"

Looking at me, Holmes said, "Watson, would you please examine the body for any writing?"

"Oh there's writing," said Hansford Worth. "There are some strange symbols in blood on the left side of the boy's abdomen."

Kneeling by the body, I slowly pulled back the sheet. On the left side of the victim's abdomen was a single stab wound just below the heart and on the right side of was a succession of figures. Although I didn't know what they meant, they looked exactly like those that had been drawn on the other bodies.

Turning to Baring-Gould, Holmes asked, "Can you translate that?"

"I'm afraid not, Mr. Holmes. I know it is ogham, and although I have spent a little time studying it, I am afraid my knowledge will not suffice in this instance."

Holmes looked at both Burnard and Hansford Worth, both of whom shook their heads.

"Watson, would you please make an exact copy of that for me? I shall have it deciphered when we return to London."

As I followed my friend's instructions, trying to reproduce the symbols with painstaking accuracy, I heard Holmes interrogating the others. "Did anyone notice any footprints near the body?"

"The grass around the body had been trampled somewhat," replied Hansford Worth, "but there were no footprints to speak of."

"Have any strangers been seen in the area lately?"

"No more than usual," said Burnard. "We always have a few amateur archaeologists examining the stone rows and the Giant's Basin."

"The Giant's Basin?" asked Holmes.

Pointing back in the direction from which we had come earlier that morning, he indicated a large mound.

"What exactly is that?" asked Holmes.

"It is a huge cairn, but many of the stones have been removed," explained Baring-Gould. "In the center is a rather large crater. We suspect that it was used as a burial ground. However, everyone agrees that the rows were here first and that the cairn was a later addition."

"Lestrade, why don't you and Inspector McKendry examine the site on the chance that it is somehow tied to the death of this young man.

"Gentlemen, perhaps you could accompany them and explain the significance of anything they might discover. Watson and I will remain here with the body. Also, Inspector McKendry, could you have someone procure a wagon so that we might transport the body. I am certain the family is going to want a proper funeral."

Pointing to the only remaining constable, McKendry said, "Crimmins, please go to Yelverton and return with a wagon of some sort."

"Very good, sir," said the constable, who started walking to the Giant's Basin with the others.

Left alone, I said to Holmes, "What was that all about?"

"I wanted the opportunity to examine the body without Lestrade peering over my shoulder," he replied.

"Well, if I can save you a bit of trouble, there appears to be a small puncture mark on the boy's right arm."

"On the arm, you say? Not the neck, like the others?"

"I didn't see one on the neck, but I must admit that I didn't look there after I had discovered the one on his arm."

Gently lifting the boy's head, Holmes began to examine the young man's neck. "Here it is," he exclaimed, "just like the others."

"What do you make of that?" I asked.

"Pressed for an answer, I should say the young man was drugged and at some point he started to regain consciousness, at which time more drugs were administered – this time in the arm."

"But why?" I said aloud. "If you are going to kill someone, why drug them beforehand?"

"Why, indeed?" replied Holmes. "Watson, as you know, I have been confronted by any number of puzzles over the course of my career. However, I must admit that I have never encountered anything quite like this. Obviously, the drugs render the victim pliant, but beyond that I am lost.

"I cannot see my way forward," said my friend in a moment of unvarnished honesty that I am certain was painful to him.

"But you will," I replied. "You always do."

"Thank you, Watson," he said. "These events just present more of a challenge because they are seemingly random. And yet, we know they are connected."

After he had examined the body and the branches thoroughly, Holmes cast his lens upon each article of the young man's clothing and the other items that had been found in the bag. I could see from the look on his face that he was no closer to the truth.

After some time, Lestrade and McKendry rejoined us.

"So have you come across anything that might help us, Mr. Holmes?" asked McKendry.

"I am sorry to report that I have no news," replied my friend. "However, you did say the young man was a baronet?"

"Yes, Mr. Holmes. Lord Deveron was the eldest son of the late Henry Deveron, Baron of Ravenhurst."

"He was killed in the Sudan Campaign, wasn't he?" I asked.'

"I believe he was," replied McKendry. "If I remember correctly he was killed during the siege of Khartoum when General Gordon and the garrison were massacred. As far as I know this was his only child."

"Has anyone informed his mother?" I asked.

"I cannot be sure," replied McKendry. "I was planning to journey to Ravenhurst tomorrow to speak with her. I am certain that by then she will have been informed of the boy's death."

"If you don't mind, Inspector, I should very much like to accompany you on that trip," said Holmes.

Lestrade glanced at me, but all I could do was shrug.

"I should be grateful for the company, Mr. Holmes," said McKendry.

"And Watson, you will accompany us," Holmes stated, rather than asked. Looking at McKendry, he said, "I think that having a medical man on hand when delivering such sad news might be to everyone's advantage."

"I agree Mr. Holmes," said McKendry.

After arrangements were made to meet the next morning, Holmes turned to Lestrade and said, "I have made a copy of the symbols on the boy's abdomen, Inspector. I should be quite grateful if you would have Dr. Steven Smith translate them. I will wire you from somewhere to ask about their meaning."

I could see from the expression on Lestrade's face that he was less than pleased with being treated as little more than an errand boy. So I wasn't totally surprised when Holmes looked at him and said simply, "A word, Inspector?"

"Of course, Mr. Holmes."

With that Holmes and Lestrade wandered off a short distance where they spent five minutes in earnest conversation. When they returned, the expressions on their faces were indecipherable. I desperately wanted to know what Holmes had said to the lawman, but I knew there was no point in pressing the issue. Holmes would tell me when he was ready.

Turning back to the group, Holmes said, "Reverend Baring-Gould, as you know there have been three sacrificial killings on three days that the ancient druids held sacred. Each has occurred at a site that predates the Romans in Britain. If you were pressed, might you hazard a guess as to a site the druids might have revered on the shortest day of the year – the winter solstice?"

"Dear me, Mr. Holmes. I should have to give that some serious thought. I should also like to consult with a few colleagues who know far more about the religious practices of the ancient Celts than I do."

"I understand," said Holmes. "Please be aware that secrecy is of paramount importance here. Who knows how far these people are willing to go to protect themselves and their heinous practices?"

"I shall be the soul of discretion, I assure you, Mr. Holmes. However, I should advise you that you there is another important druidic feast before the winter solstice."

"And that would be?" asked my friend.

"It's called Samhain or 'Winter Night,' and it occurs on the night of October 31st and carries on into the morning of November 1st."

"All Hallows Eve," exclaimed Holmes, "of course. Thank you for reminding me of that."

Chapter 12

As we made our way back to the inn, I thought I could tell from Holmes' expression that he was somewhat chagrined to have been reminded of a druidic holiday when he had been steeping himself in their culture and practices.

As we strolled along Dartmoor, I finally said to Holmes, "Did you really forget there is a druidic holiday on October 31st?"

"Not at all, old friend. In fact, that is one of the more intriguing aspects of this case."

"What is?"

"The ancient druidic calendar was divided up into eight cycles. The equinoxes and the solstices were ceremonies that revolved around the sun. However, there are four other festivals – Imbolc, Beltane, Lughnasadh and Samhain – that focus on the moon and the farming cycles. In fact, these four festivals are all Celtic in origin and those are the Celtic names. Two of them, Beltane and Lughnasadh, take their names directly from the Celtic deities, Bel and Lugh."

I must admit that I was stunned to discover the breadth of knowledge my friend had accrued regarding the druids.

"What do you find intriguing?"

"Thus far, all of the murders have taken place on the days of the solar celebrations. To the best of my knowledge, no one has been killed on any of the lunar observances."

"And the significance?"

"I am not certain yet, Watson, but I will say that the absence of killings on those days does dovetail neatly with a theory that I have been developing."

"Would you care to enlighten one who is still walking in darkness?"

"Not just yet, my friend, but I will give you an avenue to pursue if you'd like."

"By all means," I replied.

"As you know the druids have always been closely associated with nature and in particular trees. We found three yew braches placed around the body of Annie Lock, three willow branches around Jeremy Mason and now three hazel cuttings near the body of young Lord Deveron.

"May I suggest that you study the manner in which each tree was regarded by the druids? I wonder if you will arrive at the same conclusion as I."

"Well, that will have to wait until we return to London," I protested.

Looking at me, Holmes remarked, "I believe time is on our side, Watson. We know that our killer is in no hurry and that he murders his victims on very specific dates, of that I am reasonably certain. And while I should like to clap him in irons tomorrow, today if it were possible, I am forced to wait. Thus far he has given us precious little with which to work; however, I believe this latest murder may be the start of his undoing."

I was stunned to hear Holmes' remark. As we walked, I wondered if it might be a show of bravado for my benefit. I have often remarked how fond Holmes is of his little dramatic moments. However, the resolute tone of his voice and the set of his jaw told me that my friend was onto something. I knew I would learn all in due time, so for the moment, I would have to curtail my curiosity and attempt to arrive at the same conclusion as he.

Early the next morning, we met Inspector McKendry, and we traveled by rail to Bath. The ancestral home of Lord Deveron was located midway between Bristol and Bath. After arriving at the station, we procured a carriage and arrived at Ravenhurst a little after noon.

The large manor house was situated on a slight rise and afforded a panoramic view of the surrounding countryside. We saw it in the distance long before we arrived at the gatehouse to the estate.

After McKendry had identified himself to the gatekeeper, he informed us that we were expected and to proceed to the main house. The gatekeeper also told us, "You may release your cab. Her Ladyship has arranged for a carriage to return you to the rail station."

We drove along a graveled drive for at least a mile. Alongside the drive, various autumnal flowers had been planted. There were all manner of trees on the estate, with some of them already arrayed in their most brilliant fall finery. To one side, there was a stand of brilliant evergreens, their verdant display offering a stark contrast to the colorful landscape that surrounded them.

"I should like to be here at Christmastime," I remarked.

"Yes, those evergreens are quite striking are they not," remarked Holmes, "and quite young unless I miss my guess. Perhaps no more than 50 years old."

"How could you possibly know that?" I asked.

"Consider the height of the lowest branches," remarked Holmes. "If those trees were significantly older, the boughs would

73

be somewhat higher. As it is, you can easily reach up and touch the lowest branches on even the largest of them."

At length, we finally emerged from under the canopy of the trees along to the road to find ourselves in front of a classic example of an Elizabethan country house that had obviously been modeled on Hardwick Hall. Four stories tall, the structure was a marvel in that its exterior seemed more window than wall.

As we ascended the front steps, the large wooden door was opened by a servant in livery before we could knock. After McKendry told him who we were, he responded by saying, "Her Ladyship is expecting you. Please follow me."

I have been in many grand homes over the course of my career, but Ravenhurst surpassed them all. The great hall had been constructed on an axis through the center of the house rather than at right angles to the entrance. The walls were adorned with tapestries depicting hunting scenes and other portraits of pastoral life.

We ascended a switchback stairway and followed the servant through a gallery that stretched across almost the entire front of the manor. Here the walls were adorned with paintings by any number of renowned artists, including Hans Holbein the Younger, William Hogarth, Sir Joshua Reynolds and too many others to name. I cannot swear to it, but I thought I recognized a work by the poet William Blake as well.

I was surprised when I saw that Holmes had stopped and was inspecting the portrait of a rather striking woman. While he is many things, Holmes has little appreciation for the arts, and his interest in this portrait, when it was surrounded by so many other masterpieces by what I believe were far more accomplished artists, struck me as odd. I made a mental note to ask my friend about it later.

Finally, we arrived at a pair of doors, which the servant opened, and then he led us into a great chamber, at which point, the he said, "Gentlemen, please be seated. Her Ladyship will be along momentarily. I shall bring you refreshments. Please make yourselves comfortable." With that, he bowed and was gone.

I looked at Holmes and McKendry and said, "This is the grandest house that I have ever seen. I believe it could rival one of the Queen's castles."

McKendry replied, "I believe you are right, Doctor Watson. I had always wondered how the other half lived. Now, I know."

As we were talking, I saw Holmes prowling about the chamber.

"I really don't think this room gets 'lived in' a great deal," he suddenly remarked.

"Why do you say that," I asked.

"You heard the squeak of the doors when the servant opened them. I find it hard to believe that if this room were often used, they would have arrived at that state. Also, the windows in the long gallery were spotless, while these have a thin, but noticeable, coating of dust on them."

At that moment, we heard the squeak that Holmes had just alluded to, and a woman, dressed all in black, entered the room.

"Gentlemen, I am Lady Judith Deveron. I am sorry to have kept you waiting, but I needed a few moments to compose myself. Your arrival, though expected, suddenly made the horror of my son's death hit home again. I think I half expected to see Trent standing here, and I was prepared to chastise him for such a cruel prank."

I have seen many beautiful women in my life, but there was something compelling about Lady Deveron. Dressed in black, as befits a mother in mourning, she was still a vision. Tall and slender with long, dark hair and crystal blue eyes, she seemed almost fragile. I thought to myself, "A cross word from Holmes, and this woman will collapse."

"Gentlemen, please be seated," she said. "I shall do my best to answer any and all questions that you might have. I want my son's killer captured, tried and executed."

Standing there watching this brave woman, I was struck by her fierceness and her unwavering demand for justice for her slain son.

"I can certainly appreciate your agony, Your Ladyship," said Holmes. "I give you my word that I will do everything in my power to see that your wishes are carried out."

"Thank you, Mr. Holmes."

At that moment, the door opened and the servant wheeled in a tea trolley. It bore pots of coffee and tea as well as scones, clotted cream, and several types of jam.

"Gentlemen, you must be famished after your journey. There is nothing that precludes us from enjoying a light repast while I answer your questions, is there Mr. Holmes? Inspector McKendry?"

Both men shook their heads.

We watched as Her Ladyship poured the tea, and I noticed that she preferred it with lemon rather than milk and sugar. A woman after my own heart, I thought.

After taking a scone and a sip of tea, McKendry began by saying, "I might as well get right to the point. Can you think of anyone who might have wanted to harm your son, Your Ladyship?"

"No, Inspector. Trent was enormously popular – both at school and here in the village. He had a warm, generous personality, and everyone who met him thought well of him."

"Do you have any idea why he might have left the school grounds?" asked Holmes.

"None that I can think of," she replied.

"Was he doing well in school?" continued Holmes.

"He was at the top of his class and preparing for university next year," she said proudly. Suddenly, as if struck by the realization that it would never happen, she began to sob softly. After she had regained her composure, she said, "I apologize, gentlemen."

"Not at all," said Holmes solicitously. "I cannot imagine the agony you must be going through."

"We must persevere," she said.

Looking at McKendry, Holmes said, "We will take our leave, now, Your Ladyship. If anything should occur to you, please feel free to contact either Inspector McKendry or myself. And please know that you have our deepest sympathies."

As we rose, she did as well. "No need, Your Ladyship. We can see ourselves out."

"Just a moment, please," she said as she rang a small silver bell to summon the servant.

When the door opened, she said, "Thomas, our guests are leaving now. Is the carriage ready?"

"It is, Your Ladyship."

Turning back to us, she said, "Thank you for your kind words. I can only wish that we had met under different circumstances."

As we walked back through the long gallery, McKendry and I had reached the stairs before I realized that Holmes was no longer with us. Looking back, I saw him pause for a few seconds to admire a different painting. I then watched as he walked to the work, a landscape of some sort as far as I could tell, and examined it quite closely. He then turned to a maid, who was dusting, and spoke with her for a moment or two. After she had disappeared into the sitting room, Holmes quickly put his walking stick up against the painting, and I could only assume that he was attempting to measure it. After the maid had returned, Holmes spoke with her briefly. When he finally rejoined us, I thought that I detected just the slightest smile on his face. I was about to ask him about it, when he shook his head as a signal to me to be quiet.

On the ride back to the station, Holmes was silent, and I could tell that he was deep in thought. Knowing his moods, I began to converse with McKendry and soon discovered that we had several interests in common, including the turf. While we sat there debating how the prince's horse, Diamond Jubilee, might fare in the upcoming Middle Park Stakes in October, Holmes sat silently, pondering the events of the day. I could see from his posture that some small degree of progress had been made.

At the station, after the servant had departed, and McKendry had boarded his train for home, we were finally alone. Looking at my friend, I remarked, "What a remarkable woman, to have borne her sorrow with such dignity."

"Yes, Watson, I agree. I should say that determination and resolve are two of her more outstanding characteristics."

"She did her best to help," I said, "until she was overcome with grief."

"As always, you hit the mark, Watson. Although I was impressed by what she did tell us, I was struck even more by what she failed to communicate."

I was about to ask what he meant by that remark when I heard a train whistle in the distance.

"We should be back in London by early evening," Holmes stated.

"Do you have a pressing matter?"

"I intend to pay yet another visit to the British Museum as I have several things about which I must speak with Dr. Connors as soon as possible, and then after I have concluded my business with him, it is possible that I may need to speak with one of their curators about a painting."

"Was there a clue in one of the paintings?"

"It was right there in front of you, Watson, in Her Ladyship's Long Gallery."

Looking at my friend, I remarked before he could, "Yes, I know. Once again, I saw but I did not observe."

Chapter 13

The next morning, I awoke to find that Holmes had already eaten. I found him sitting in his chair poring over the morning papers.

"Well, they are certainly making the most of this latest slaying," he remarked.

"The press?"

"Yes, look at this headline, 'Deadly druid strikes again.' What poppycock!" he remarked.

"I suppose, but headlines do sell papers."

"Yes, I suppose they do, but they also terrify people."

"Well, then you must put a stop to the killings."

"I am trying my friend, but we are up against a very clever adversary. They have covered their tracks quite carefully, leaving me precious little with which to work. The only thing we know for certain is the date of the next killing. However, I must confess that I think I can discern a faint light at the end of the tunnel."

"Would you care to enlighten me?"

"Bravo, Watson. Like the Bard, you will pursue your puns."

At that moment, there was a knock on the door. "Come in," said Holmes. A young lad, whom I thought I recognized as one of Holmes' street Arabs, entered and said, "Here's the note from Dr. Connors, sir." He then handed my friend an envelope.

"Thank you Daniel."

"Will there be anything else, sir?' asked the boy.

"Not at the moment, no. But tell the Irregulars I may require their services in the very near future." With that Holmes handed the youngster some coins.

"Thank you, Mr. Holmes," said the boy who then snapped to attention like a young soldier and saluted my friend before bounding down the stairs and slamming the front door.

Opening the note, Holmes read it over and then looking at me said, "Dr. Connors is free until one o'clock and then he will be in meetings until four. He says come when it is convenient, either before or after his meeting. I am rather anxious to discuss several points with him, so I'm going to see him now. Would you care to accompany me, old friend?"

"Just let me get my coat," I remarked.

We took a cab to the British Museum and were soon ushered into the office of Professor Connors. A tall, slender man, Connors was wearing a dark blue suit, with a white shirt and an old school tie that told me he had attended Cambridge. He wore silver glasses, but the intelligence in his piercing blue eyes was obvious, and his smile was warm and genuine.

I was feeling rather proud of my deductions when I heard Holmes say, "Thank you for seeing us on such short notice, Professor Connors. This is my colleague, Dr. John Watson."

"Not at all, Mr. Holmes. Anything I can do to help, I certainly will."

"Your meeting this morning, I assume that you received the budget increase that you were seeking?"

"How could you possibly know about that?" he replied in amazement.

"Come, come, Professor. It's written all over you. Today, you are wearing your best suit, your shoes have been polished to a dazzling luster and your necktie has been tied in a full Windsor, father than the simple four-in-hand knot that has been your wont."

"You amaze me, Mr. Holmes."

"Well, do give your wife my best and tell her that should I ever have need of such a knot, I shall call upon her for assistance."

"How could you possibly know that my wife tied this tie?"

"On your shoulder is a single long red hair. I can only suppose that it ended up there when she was assisting you with your preparations."

"I give up, Mr. Holmes. You are right about the suit, the tie and my wife," said Connors as he plucked the strand of hair from his shoulder. "But how on Earth, could you know that I was at a budget meeting?"

"A man in your position very seldom has to put on airs. You are well-respected; you have been with the museum for more than 20 years, so there is no chance that your job is in jeopardy. That led me to the inevitable conclusion that you must be discussing finances. Also, your secretary's desk is groaning under the weight of stacks of documents, all of which are filled with columns of figures."

"It seems so simple when you explain it," laughed Connors.

"That's why a magician never explains how his tricks are done," said Holmes. "The mystery rests in the creation of the illusion."

"Don't you worry about it, Professor; he does it to me all the time," I said.

"Now, to business," said Holmes. "I am certain that you have heard of the murder of the young baronet on Dartmoor."

"I have Mr. Holmes. Did you meet the Reverend Baring-Gould? Was he of any assistance?"

"In his own way, he was enormously helpful," said my friend. "Now that we have three murders, is there anything that links the locales beyond the fact that all the bodies were found at historical sites – some or all of which may have been connected to druids?"

"I do not think so, Mr. Holmes. The locations, like the victims, appear to have been chosen quite at random. All of the sites are thousands of years old, but I have been able to find nothing that would seem to link them.

"Stonehenge served as some sort of calendar for the ancients. That we know. However, neither the White Horse nor 'The Bone' has any sort of functionality associated with it – unless of course, you consider that 'The Bone' may have been used as a burial site. Still the Giant's Basin, a huge cairn, is located quite close by, so I rather doubt that functionality is the key."

"Yes, I'm inclined to agree with you there," said Holmes. "I wonder though if either the victims or the sites were truly chosen at random," he added.

"Which brings us right back to where we started," I interjected.

"No, Watson, as I told you. I can see faint glimmerings at the end of the tunnel, but I'm afraid we must stumble around in the darkness for quite some time before we arrive at true illumination.

"As you know, yew branches had been placed about the first body, willow about the second and hazel about the third. Have you been able to learn anything about the significance of the trees?"

"I've been researching the various trees, Mr. Holmes," said Connors, "and I think I have come across a few interesting facts. The yew tree, an evergreen, was regarded by both the druids and later the Christians as a symbol of everlasting life."

"That would seem to place the significance of the yew branches at odds with the ogham writing on her torso," said Holmes, thinking aloud more than making conversation.

"Yes, didn't the symbols translate to the word 'death'?" I asked.

"Indeed, they did," said Holmes.

"That may be explained," said Connors. "There are many references to yews in Irish and Scottish poems and they are often described in connection with churchyards." He paused and began rummaging through some papers on his desk. Finding the one he sought, he read a bit and then said, "The naturalist Gilbert White, who also happened to be a parson, described the trees as 'an emblem of mortality by their funereal appearance.'"

"If memory serves," said Holmes, "White died sometime in the 1790s."

"I believe you are right, Mr. Holmes," said Connors.

"Is that important?" I asked.

"It may prove to be, but right now, it is too soon to say," said Holmes. Turning back to Connors, he asked, "Can you tell me anything about the other two branches?"

"Indeed," replied Connors. "The willow is one of the seven sacred Irish trees and is also sacred to druids, both past and present. Oddly enough, the willow is often regarded as the first to arrive –

a symbol of spring – and the last to leave – a symbol of winter. I would be hard-pressed to explain why willow branches were placed about the body found on the summer solstice."

"But might there be an explanation?" pressed Holmes.

"Well, the willow is associated with the letter S. Within the ogham writing, Saille is the lunar month; numerologically, it is related to the number five. So I suppose the phrase summer solstice, both words beginning with S, might explain its appearance."

"Yes, but the summer solstice would be more accurately referred to as midsummer, would it not?" asked Holmes.

"That's true," said Connors. "The early calendars had but two seasons – summer and winter. The seasons began and ended on the equinoxes, so the solstices would be the midpoints – midsummer and midwinter – even though midsummer truly doesn't occur until August and midwinter until January."

"I believe that we are making definite progress," exclaimed Holmes.

Totally befuddled, I decided to keep my confusion to myself.

"Finally, we come to the hazel," said Holmes.

Waxing eloquent, Connors began, "The hazel might be said to be the quintessential Celtic tree because of its position at the heart of the Otherworld. According to myth, nine magic hazel trees hang over the Well of Wisdom and drop their purple nuts into the water. There are many references to drinking 'hazelmead' in early Irish literature and to Scottish druids eating hazel nuts to gain the power of prophecy.

"The hazel was sacred to the god Thor in Germanic mythology while the Greeks and Romans saw the tree as sacred to Hermes and Mercury respectively," continued Connors.

"That's all well and good, Professor Connors," said Holmes, "but has the tree any association with the autumnal equinox that you know of?"

"No, Mr. Holmes. Most commonly throughout the centuries, the hazel has been used as a protection against evil. While the hazel is frequently mentioned throughout the mythological landscape, I have not been able to find any direct associations with that particular day."

"Thank you very much, Professor Connors. You have shed even more light on a dark problem."

"Have I?" he asked.

"Indeed, you have," exclaimed Holmes. After shaking his hand warmly, Holmes said, "I cannot thank you enough. I shall let you know when my investigation bears fruit."

When we were in the hall, Holmes turned to me and said, "Surely, you see the pattern?"

"I must confess, old man, that it escapes me."

"Well, keep mulling over what Professor Connors told us about the branches. I am certain it will come to you."

"Holmes, I must confess, I cannot see the forest, nor the trees, let alone the branches."

"You sell yourself short, my friend. I must go to Oxford. Would you care to accompany me?"

Since I had several errands to run and had promised a colleague that I would be available to cover his practice, should he need me, I apologized to my friend, and told him that I would see him in the evening.

With that, Holmes descended the steps in front of the museum. The last I saw of my friend that day, he was entering a cab which soon departed in the direction of Paddington.

I spent part of the afternoon at my solicitor's office and then dined alone as my colleague had no need of my services. I considered taking in "The Gipsy Earl" at the Adelphi, but then decided that I would rather wait and see what news, if any, Holmes might be bearing.

It was nearing nine when I heard my friend's familiar tread ascending the stairs. He entered the room and his face bore a slight smile. I could tell that his efforts had yielded some fruit, but knowing his flair for the dramatic, I decided to indulge him and let him spin his tale in his own time.

After hanging up his coat, he looked at me and smiled. Then he said quite casually, "So how did your visit with your solicitor go?"

Although I am used to Holmes doing that sort of thing, I must admit that I was stunned that had been able to ascertain my whereabouts. Deciding to play along, I said, "I'm going to take you at your word that you traveled to Oxford today."

"I did," he replied, thoroughly enjoying my confused state.

"And I'm going to trust that you had no one following me, just so you could perform your little parlor trick."

"On my word, I did not."

"Then how on Earth could you possibly know that I visited Dougherty today? I have changed my clothes since I returned home. There is no mud on my boots or ink stains on my cuff. And the papers that he gave me have been placed in my strongbox under my bed. There are no clues, I say. So how could you possibly know?"

"You may have changed my clothes, my friend, but you have not changed your habits."

"What on Earth are you talking about?"

"I have thrice accompanied you to your solicitor's office in the past. Each time I watched amused as you placed a handful of the sweets that his secretary keeps in a dish in your pocket as she announced your presence. So when I see the ashtray next to your sitting chair, containing the wrappers from such confections, what else can I conclude?

"You concealed your legal papers, but not your confectionary papers," he laughed.

"Holmes, you astound me!"

"Nothing to it, old man."

"So, given your somewhat lighter mood, can I surmise that your trip was a successful one?"

"We are getting closer, Watson, but knowing and proving are two very different things, as you know."

"What drew you to Oxford, Holmes?"

"Over the past few months, I have been making inquiries regarding anything concerning the druids. Surprisingly, I learned about a painting depicting the ancient Celtic priests."

"A painting, you say? Is it prehistoric? And if so how does it figure into these dastardly killings?"

Holmes chuckled, "No, it's a fairly contemporary work. As for whether it ties into the murders, I believe that it may. I still have some sorting out to do in that area," he said ruefully.

"What painting? Surely you could have found something similar here in one of the London museums?"

"I think not, Watson. The painting is titled 'A Converted British Family Sheltering a Christian Missionary from the Persecution of the Druids' by William Holman Hunt."

"I believe that I have heard of the fellow," I said.

"I am certain that you have. Together with John Everett Millais and Dante Gabriel Rosetti, he founded a group called the Pre-Raphelite Brotherhood. They believed that Raphael's classical poses combined with his emphasis on elegant composition had corrupted the academic teaching of art. But I digress, you want to hear about my trip not the artistic squabbles that surround us.

"At any rate, Millais had painted a work which he titled 'Christ in the House of His Parents.' The work is replete with religious symbolism as the family tends to the wound that a young Jesus has suffered. More to our line is the fact that Hunt painted his 'Persecution of the Druids' as a companion piece.

"It's an interesting work in that, as its title suggests, an early British family of Christians is providing refuge for one missionary in a rather primitive hut. Outside, in the background, a mob of pagans, urged on by a druid is attempting to capture a second missionary. Again the work is rife with religious symbols, including a cross painted in red on one of stones in the hut. Even more interesting, however, is that sections of a stone circle can be seen through the openings of the hut."

"A stone circle?"

"Yes, rather like a miniature Stonehenge," offered Holmes. "It is suggestive, is it not?"

"It is curious," I remarked.

"Both Millais' and Hunt's works now hang in the Ashmolean Museum of Art and Archaeology in Oxford.

"Even more curious is the fact that while Millais' work has been hanging there since it was painted, Hunt's work was donated to the museum about five months ago."

"Just before the second killing, I exclaimed. "If we can find out who donated it that may point us in the direction of the killer."

"That is going to prove an extremely difficult task," said Holmes.

"Why do you say that?"

"I visited the museum about two months ago, and the curator told me that he woke one morning and arrived at work only to discover the painting had been placed on his desk sometime during the night.

"It had been carefully wrapped in blankets and paper. Attached to it was a note that read 'Companion pieces belong together.'

"As you might expect, the blankets, paper and note were not preserved. Oh Watson," he said vehemently, "those items might have told us a great deal about who owned the painting prior to the museum. They might have even been used as evidence against our killer."

"Well, surely, Hunt must know to whom he sold the painting," I added.

"We will find out tomorrow," said Holmes, "but something tells me this trail of breadcrumbs is going to end very soon."

Chapter 14

The next morning Holmes had once again breakfasted and left our lodgings by the time I arose. I caught up on my correspondence and then lunched at my club. When I returned to Baker Street in the early afternoon, I found Holmes sitting in his chair and the room filled with smoke from his pipe.

"How did your morning go?" I asked.

"I am afraid to report that things could have gone significantly better," he said. "'Persecution of the Druids' was Hunt's first major work. He exhibited the painting in 1850 at the Royal Academy where it was purchased by William Bennet as a gift for the late Thomas Combe, who subsequently became Hunt's patron and benefactor. When Combe died, the estate passed to his wife, and after her death in 1893, the bulk of the collection they had amassed was bequeathed to the Ashmolean Museum.

"Apparently, the druid painting did not go the museum at that time, but no one seems to know who possessed the work until it turned up at the museum some several months ago."

"How is that possible?"

"The solicitor who had handled the estate has passed, and apparently he was not the most fastidious at keeping records."

"Have you any idea where it went?"

"I have very definite suspicions," replied Holmes. "However just as there is an ocean of uncertainty between suspecting and knowing, so too is there an equally wide gulf between knowing and proving.

"I am reasonably certain that I know who acquired the painting; however, proving my theory may require a great deal of legwork and a bit of luck. And even if I could prove where the painting had been residing, there is no way to prove that its owner is our killer."

"No way? Are you certain?"

"Well, I am not entirely certain of a great many things about this case, my friend, but I cannot let my doubts hinder my investigation. Three murders have been committed, and unless I miss my guess, a fourth will take place, unless we can somehow prevent it. Someone must stand for those deaths, and it falls to us, old friend, to see that justice is done."

"You can count on me, Holmes!"

"Good old, Watson!" he exclaimed. "Here is what I would like you to do, if you are willing."

"I am yours to command, my friend."

"First, I should like you to visit both the Ancient Order of Druids and the United Ancient Order of Druids. Despite the similar sounding names, they are two very different organizations, I assure you. See if any of their members has been acting rather strangely of late. More to the point, see if any members have come and gone within the past year. I have visited both groups in disguise, as you know, but I believe that the membership might best be described as 'fluid.'"

"That doesn't seem particularly difficult," I remarked.

"Never take anything for granted, my friend, especially where murder is concerned."

"Of course, you are right," I replied. "Anything else?"

"Do you remember what Connors said about the branches seeming not to match with the seasons in which the murders were committed?"

"I do."

"If you can find a member that seems knowledgeable about the ancient druids and whom you think you can trust, see if he is willing to verify Connors' beliefs. It's not that I doubt the man, but I would rather have the information authenticated by an actual believer, so to speak.

"Finally, try to learn if the local druids are planning anything for All Hallows Eve, or as they call it Samhain."

I was jotting down Holmes' instructions in my notebook, and when I had finished, I looked at him and said, "Anything else?"

"Not at the moment," he said.

"And what will you be doing whilst I am steeping myself in druidic lore?"

"I shall be revisiting each of the murder scenes. Tomorrow, I leave for Salisbury, from there I will make connections to Uffington and then once more to Dartmoor."

"I expect to be away at least four and possibly five days, so I am counting on you to keep me apprised of any new developments, should they occur."

"How am I to do that?"

"I shall be staying at the Old Post House in Salisbury, if you desire to contact me. From there, I will make my way to Yelverton and take a room at the same inn that we used on our last visit. As for Dartmoor, I am going to wire the Reverend Baring-Gould and inquire as to whether I might impose upon his hospitality for a night. His estate is Lew Trenchard, and it is approximately 20 miles from the stone rows. So there you have my itinerary."

"Are you sure you don't want me to accompany you?" I asked. "There is safety in numbers."

"That is certainly true," replied Holmes, "but to quote your Mr. Kipling,

'Down to Gehenna or up to the Throne,

He travels the fastest, who travels alone.'"

To say that my feelings were hurt would be something of an understatement. And then I remembered that we were in pursuit of a cold-blooded killer. I had been given my orders, and, by God, I would carry them out.

I guess Holmes must have seen the look of disappointment on my face, for he added, "There is one other reason that you cannot accompany me, old friend."

"Oh?"

"Yes, I shall be traveling incognito, and I shall be using the name Alf Stimson. So any wires for me should be addressed to that name."

Knowing Holmes' fondness for disguises and his uncanny ability to breathe life into the characters he created, I felt better immediately.

"And pray tell, what does this Alf Stimson do to earn his keep?"

"A little of this, and a little of that, he's a very adaptable fellow," laughed Holmes.

"Now, would you care for a sherry before dinner?"

* * *

Once again, Holmes had departed before I had risen the next morning. After breakfast and running a few errands, I made my way to the United Ancient Order of Druids, which had split off from the Ancient Order of Druids some sixty years ago.

I wasn't quite certain exactly what I would find, but I was determined to carry out Holmes' request. Of the several members with whom I spoke, few knew much about the group that had given their organization its name.

To a man they insisted, that their group which was run by an elected board of directors, existed primarily for "social and intellectual intercourse" as well as "general philanthropy and benevolence." They pointed to such charitable exercises as caring for out-of-work members and assisting with the funeral expenses of the impoverished in their ranks as among the organization's many endeavors. They could shed little light on any modern-day druids acting out of sorts. However, I did learn that they had a benefit dance planned for All Hallows Eve.

Deciding that little if anything was to be learned there, I made way to the King's Arms on Poland Street in Soho. This was where the Ancient Order of Druids had been founded in Britain in 1781. I encountered several men who claimed to be members, but none would discuss any of their practices with me.

I was feeling frustrated when a young man approached. He introduced himself as Gerald Massey, saying "I know who you are and I can guess why you are here, but this is not the place for such a discussion."

Since he seemed to be the only one willing to talk to me, I followed him to a nearby pub at his suggestion. He began the conversation by informing me, "Our order is not a religious organization. Truth be told, Doctor Watson, any and all discussions concerning religion or politics are forbidden within our lodge rooms.

"I suspect that given our name, you were hoping to see men in robes huddled over a fire trying to divine the future. I am sorry to disappoint you, but our members are expected to try to preserve and practice the major principles attributed to the early druids, including the virtues of justice, benevolence and friendship."

"Sounds a bit like the Freemasons," I suggested.

"We have more in common than you might suspect," replied Massey.

Although he couldn't or wouldn't provide an exact number of members, he assured me that there had been no new members admitted for more than a year, and the only members who failed to attend meetings were those who had passed away.

Deciding to press on, I asked him if he knew anything about the original druids.

"Quite a great deal," he replied. "I am a poet by trade and I have studied the Romantics and found their works and their love of nature to be no small source of inspiration. It's not a great leap of faith from a healthy respect for Nature to an admiration and perhaps emulation of those who venerated the same."

He then proceeded to wax eloquent about Wordsworth and his compatriots which was followed by a rather elaborate history of London, which he claimed was a thriving druidic center in the millennia before Christ. Suffice to say that while some may find it interesting, I will not burden my readers with this rather fanciful retelling of long-ago events that had obviously been reshaped to coincide with his own rather pointed ideology.

Despite his self-professed knowledge of the ancient druids, he knew nothing about the significance of any of the tree branches.

Having visited both groups and come away knowing little more than before I had begun, I was forced to concur with Holmes' initial assessment that these druids were far more concerned with sharing a pint than sacrificing to the gods of old.

As a result, all I could do was wait until Holmes had returned from his lengthy sojourn and hope that he had fared better than I.

I spent the next few days waiting to hear from Holmes, but there were no wires nor messages. I did send a cable to Lew Trenchard informing my friend that my inquiries had come a cropper.

On that Friday afternoon, I returned to our rooms shortly before dinner time to find a visitor waiting for me. He was a tall, rather distinguished-looking gentleman, dressed all in tweeds, with elaborate mutton-chop whiskers and the fullest head of bright red hair that I have ever seen. He stood when I entered the room and introduced himself as Professor Joseph Delanèy – "accent grave over the second e," he informed me – and proclaimed himself an expert on all things druidical. (Given that pronouncement, I was wondering whether this fellow knew the difference between Gallic and Gaelic.)

"Your landlady said that I might wait in this room. I received a letter from Mr. Holmes instructing me to be here at this hour," he explained. "He seems keenly interested in some archaeological work that I am conducting in Brittany."

"Were there druids in France, too?" I inquired.

"Absolutely, Doctor. Have you never heard of the Carnac Stones?"

"Can't say that I have," I replied.

"They are one of the most extensive menhir collections in the world," he replied. "Simply magnificent."

"Well, that's more Holmes' department than mine," I said. "However, I think Mr. Holmes is focusing his attention on British stone circles. I can't say that French circles would fit into the scope of his investigation."

Suddenly, the man's voice changed as he said, "One should never dismiss any information just because it doesn't appear to fit into a preconceived notion. You should know better than that Watson."

To my chagrin, I realized that Professor Delanèy was Holmes in one of his many disguises and that I had once again been duped by my friend. "That wasn't very kind of you," I said, with a note of irritation in my voice. "Besides, you told me you were traveling as Alf Stimson. Whatever happened to that fellow?"

"He outlived his usefulness," remarked Holmes as he began to remove his makeup. "He proved himself quite useful at Salisbury and Uffington, but I had to leave Alf behind when I visited the Reverend Baring-Gould, and he would have been totally out of place at Exeter and Lady Deveron's estate, hence the incarnation of Professor Delanèy."

"Well, that's all well and good," I replied, "but have you learned anything of substance."

"Quite a great deal, actually," replied Holmes. "We inch ever closer to the truth, and if my suspicions are correct, this is a far more sordid business than even I had suspected."

"What have you discovered?"

"I learned that Annie Locke was little more than a child. She had made few friends during her short stay in Salisbury although there were rumors that she was seeing one of the town's young swains."

"And was she?" I asked.

"Indeed! She was also saving her money for her trip to Canada. She hadn't an enemy in the world so far as I can tell, and everyone with whom I spoke is at a loss to explain her rather grim demise."

"And how about young Jeremy Mason?"

"Again, I spoke with his parents and acquaintances, while disguised as Alf, and their stories remain pretty much the same. There were a few minor discrepancies, but I attribute those to the passage of time. Had those I questioned been involved, their stories would have been learned by rote and not a single detail would have been altered.

"Jeremy had few friends and appears to have been very much the outlier. I think that partially explains his selection by our killer. Jeremy was probably thrilled with the prospect of finally making a friend, and then he was betrayed in a most heinous manner."

"How did you get these people to open up to you?"

"It was quite simple," explained Holmes. "In my guise as an itinerant peddler, people are always willing to talk. They know I won't gossip or reveal their secrets because I won't be around long enough. Everyone has a story to tell, Watson. Many are just waiting for a willing audience."

"Bravo, Holmes! And what did you learn at Drizzlecombe?"

"After consulting with various experts, the Reverend Baring-Gould agrees with Professor Connors that the branches used at each killing are singularly inappropriate. He wouldn't go so far as to call them 'wrong' because there is so much we don't know about the druids."

"As I said in my wire, I'm afraid I wasn't much help there, old man. I visited both societies, and most of the members seem more concerned with socializing than anything else."

Holmes laughed at my assessment and then inquired, "Have you nothing to add?"

"I'm afraid not although I did meet one rather interesting fellow, who bent my ear with his rather farfetched tales of druids in London before Christ and the veneration of nature by the Romantic poets."

"I see you encountered Mr. Massey. He can be quite the orator when you touch on one of his favorite subjects, I met him during my first visits," said Holmes. "I was in disguise, so he wouldn't know me if he saw me. Thank heavens for small favors."

"You said you stopped at Exeter?"

"Yes. I made inquiries about Lord Deveron and discovered that he appears to have been well-liked to a rather small degree, both by his fellow students and a number of faculty members, but I would never go so far as to call him 'popular'."

"Well, we rather knew that, didn't we?"

"Yes, but we didn't know that he was constantly at odds with his mother."

"At odds, you say. What child isn't at odds with his parents at some point?"

"I suppose they all are," said Holmes, "but what makes this far more interesting is the fact that the present Lady Deveron is not his real mother. It seems that he was the product of the union between Lord Deveron and his first wife. After her untimely death, and his Lordship's remarriage, she took upon herself to raise the boy as her own."

"And what is wrong with that?"

"Nothing at all," said Holmes, "but you will recall when we left her estate I remarked to you that what she didn't say was far more interesting that what she had said."

"What am I missing?"

"She constantly referred to young man as her son rather than her stepson?"

"You suspected she was not his mother?" I asked incredulously.

"You have heard of Gregor Mendel?"

"I am familiar with the name, although I cannot say that I fully embrace all of his conclusions."

"I have studied his work, and I may try my own hand at a monograph some day on the possibility of criminal tendencies being inherited. But, I digress. Right now, some of the leading minds in Europe are re-examining his principles with an eye toward finally according the good monk his due. In fact, there is a theory that eye color is an inherited trait."

"What of it?"

"It's just that Lord Deveron had blue eyes as does Lady Judith, but the baronet had brown eyes, which if you believe the research, would eliminate her as his birth mother. Lord Deveron's first wife had brown eyes."

"How did you discover that?"

"I examined her portrait which is still hanging in the Long Gallery."

"But why conceal that?"

"Why indeed?" mused Holmes. "I think when we have an answer to that question, we may be even closer to identifying our mysterious killer."

I was about to ask Holmes about the other painting that he had examined when I caught sight of a letter that had arrived for him. "Speaking of mysterious," I said, "this was delivered for you yesterday."

I handed Holmes a long white envelope. On the outside, his name had been very carefully printed.

He examined it and then asked, "When and how did it arrive? The envelope tells me nothing as it is common stock and since there is no stamp, I can only assume it was delivered by hand."

"Yes, Mrs. Hudson found it slipped under the front door around four o'clock."

Taking a letter opener he very carefully slit the top of the envelope. He then pulled out a single sheet of white paper that had been neatly folded in half. Upon opening it, he looked at me and remarked. "I think we may be getting a little too close for someone's comfort."

"What is the message?"

"I haven't the foggiest idea of what the message says as it has been written in ogham. Here, see for yourself."

Holmes then handed me the paper. It contained but a single line of carefully written characters. I have reproduced them below.

"However, I believe that I can translate it. I had Doctor Smith prepare a page that contains the ogham alphabet with the translation of each of their symbols into an English letter."

"Holmes, you amaze me."

"Nothing to it, my friend. I anticipated encountering future ogham characters and thought the ability to translate them myself might prove invaluable." With that he began his transcription.

After a short while, I could contain myself no longer, "So what does it say?

"Just another minute or two," he said.

I watched as Holmes compared the characters to the list that had been prepared for him. After he had finished transcribing the message, he looked at me and repeated his earlier sentiment. "Yes, I think we are definitely getting too close for someone's comfort."

"What on Earth does it say?" I demanded.

Pausing for a second, Holmes then looked up at me and remarked, "The gods must be satisfied."

Chapter 15

The next morning, as were breakfasting, there was a knock on the door.

"Yes, Mrs. Hudson?" asked Holmes.

Our landlady poked her head in the door and announced, "Inspector Lestrade is here to see you, Mr. Holmes."

"Show him in, by all means," said Holmes.

A moment later, we were joined at the table by Lestrade. After a cup of tea and a bit of small talk, Lestrade said, "I'll come clean, Mr. Holmes. I have people to whom I must answer, and they want to know what we are doing to solve these murders."

"I assure you, Lestrade, that I am doing everything within my power to see justice done. I will tell you that I think I have made some small degree of progress, and I am currently exploring several promising avenues of inquiry. I will also tell you that I think there will be at least one more murder on the winter solstice unless we can find a way to prevent it."

"If this killer strikes again, I may find myself demoted," moaned Lestrade.

"Hopefully, it will not come to that," said Holmes. Tell your superiors that the net is slowly closing around this killer. If he strikes one more time, and I fully believe that he will, we will have him.

"Assure those demanding action that you are doing everything in your power to prevent another murder, and if all else fails, simply remind them that the Ripper struck more often, killing five women in less than 10 weeks – and no one was ever arrested."

"They won't like to hear that, Mr. Holmes," said Lestrade.

"The truth isn't always pleasant, my friend."

"Need we worry about All Hallows Eve as Baring-Gould suggested?" asked Lestrade.

"I hope not," said Holmes. "These killings are druidical to a degree, and thus far they have taken place on the equinoxes and the solstice. That leaves us some time to prepare for the next murder."

"But didn't the Reverend Baring-Gould say that Halloween was one of their most important celebrations?" asked Lestrade.

"Not Halloween but Samhain, although it is celebrated on the same day as our youngsters celebrate Halloween. According to the druidic calendar, Samhain is actually the end of the harvest season and the beginning of winter – the darker half of the year, if you will – and that is what gives me pause."

"If we have another murder on All Hallows Eve, my superiors will give me more than pause," remarked Lestrade.

"Then you must prepare them for the worst. Tell them thus far, the killings have occurred on the solar cycle of the druidic calendar, and there is no evidence of interest in the lunar cycle."

Lestrade looked at me quizzically.

And then Holmes continued, "Prepare them for the possibility of another killing, possibly two more, but tell them – no, guarantee them – that the killer will be captured."

"I trust you, Mr. Holmes. You've never let me down yet."

"Thank you, Lestrade. I promise you that I will do all that I may to prove that your confidence in me has not been misplaced."

After Lestrade had left, I said, "That was kind of you to bolster Lestrade's spirits like that."

"I meant every word I said," replied Holmes. "I will see this killer captured and justice done. I just hope that my efforts to prove his guilt do not come at the cost of any more human lives."

"But you didn't tell him about the letter."

"He has enough to worry about," said Holmes. "The letter is merely another diversion."

"Were you able to learn anything from it?"

"The paper was cheap, and it was written by a quill dipped in ink. The author took great pains to ensure its clarity. I believe that it was written by a man. Given the indentations of the characters in the paper, I should think he is quite strong, and he is left-handed."

"Left-handed, how on earth could you know that?"

"There is a very slight incline in all the characters from right to left. That is characteristic of those who write with their left hand. There is also a slight inclination in the backward direction. By contrast, those who are right-handed tend to write from left to right and their letters are inclined slightly forward. Although he has attempted to disguise his writing, those traits are readily discernable to the trained eye."

* * *

Over the next few weeks, Holmes divided his time between working on the druid killings, as we had come to call them, and several other affairs that demanded his attention.

I found myself quite busy covering for a colleague who had fallen ill, and so it was that I returned to Baker Street on the evening of October 28th to find Holmes conducting another of his malodorous chemical experiments. Looking up, he inquired of me, "Watson, can you clear your schedule for the next few days?"

"I suppose so," I replied, "Dr. Semler seems much better, and I am certain that he can find another locum as long as I let him know right away."

"Please do so," said Holmes. "I will tell you this, I have no definite plans at present, but three days hence is All Hallows Eve, the feast of Samhain, in the druidic calendar, so I have put myself at Lestrade's disposal. I have no idea what, if anything, he will require of me, but I gave the man my word."

"And I gave you mine. We started this together, and we will see it through."

It was around 6 in the evening when Mrs. Hudson knocked on the door. At Holmes' bidding, she opened it and informed us that Inspector Lestrade wished to see Mr. Holmes. After he had entered and seated himself, he said, "Mr. Holmes, I have been doing my homework. I know that there are many places throughout the kingdom, but I think you will agree with me that few were more highly regarded by the ancients than Avebury."

"I certainly can't argue with that Inspector," replied Holmes.

"I plan to take a few select officers, in plainclothes of course, and set out for Wiltshire on a special train from Paddington this afternoon," he said.

"I should advise against that," said Holmes.

"But why?" asked Lestrade.

"What better way to announce that something unusual is going on in a rather remote area than by having a special pull into Swindon and then having a group of strangers descend on the hamlet of Avebury. No, Lestrade, it simply won't do."

"What would you suggest, Mr. Holmes."

"Take four men and we will make seven."

"Only four?" asked Lestrade.

"Any more and we might have more officers there than there are villagers," replied Holmes.

"Have two of your men start for Swindon and the other two should head for Marlborough. They should leave as soon as possible. I would prefer that they travel alone rather than in pairs. They can pose as itinerant salesmen, chimney sweeps and peddlers. Once in the area, they can make their way to Avebury by different means. Some may rent a horse at Swindon; others may hire a carriage. It's a distance of about 10 miles. After they have arrived, have them reconnoiter the village and the surrounding areas. Are you familiar with the stone circles there, Lestrade?"

"Probably not as familiar as you are Mr. Holmes."

"There is one large circle that encloses two other, smaller circles. Nearby are other prehistoric structures, including West Kennet Long Barrow, The Sanctuary and the rather mysterious Silbury Hill."

"Blimey, Mr. Holmes, that's going to require a great many more men than I can muster on such short notice."

"If I may ask, Lestrade. Why are you focusing on Avebury?"

"You recall Mr. Holmes that I was at Avebury when the second killing took place at the Uffington White Horse."

"Yes," I interrupted, "that was the night that Holmes and I spent at the wretched Nine Ladies place."

"I am sorry about that, Doctor," said Lestrade. Turning back to my friend, he said, "Call it a policeman's hunch, Mr. Holmes, but there's something about Avebury that has haunted me since I was there. If I were this druid killer, I would find it impossible not to offer a sacrifice at that place. It is one of the queerest spots I have ever seen."

"Again, I cannot fault your deductions, Lestrade. Nor would I be inclined to argue with your finely honed instincts."

I cast a glance at Holmes, but it was impossible to tell if he were being serious or enjoying a gentle just at Lestrade's benefit.

"Now, run along, and try to get your men in place. Stress to them the importance of being inconspicuous. Also, if you have any officers who are not from London originally, you might consider assigning them. Too many similar accents, might cause someone to get the wind up."

"I've stolen a march on you there, Mr. Holmes," said Lestrade. "The same thought struck me, and I have acted accordingly."

"Bravo," said Holmes warmly. "We will make a proper inspector of you yet, Lestrade.

"So then it is settled. Watson and I will meet you at Paddington tomorrow where we shall board the four o'clock train for Swindon."

"Thank you, Mr. Holmes. I am in your debt."

After he had left, I looked at Holmes and said, "Do you really expect something to happen at Avebury?"

"Honestly, no. But if something should occur, we will be there before the townspeople and those living in the vicinity have had a chance to trample any clues underfoot that might have been left behind."

October 31st dawned bright and crisp. It grew gradually warmer to the point where it seemed more like early summer than the middle of autumn. Reflecting that today was also the first day of winter according to the druids, I had to conclude that our calendar appeared far more accurate, if that term could be applied, than theirs.

Holmes was in one of his more reticent moods. I know that he thought spending the night at Avebury was pointless, but he had given Lestrade his word. As the day wore on, Holmes became slightly more talkative, but his misgivings were written all over his face.

We met Lestrade at Paddington and had a first-class carriage on the train to Swindon. During the journey, Holmes inquired about where Lestrade planned to place his men.

"As you know, the largest stone circle is bisected by two roads that meet in the center of the village. I had thought to place one man in the North Circle, another in the South Circle. I was planning on having another patrolling the Sanctuary and I will take my spot at Silbury Hill with the last officer and then wander from site to site. I was rather hoping that you and Doctor Watson might take the West Kennet Long Barrow. Of all the places in Avebury, that would be the one where I feel our killer might strike."

"Because it has served as a burial area in the past?" asked Holmes.

"Exactly," said Lestrade. "There are plenty of places for you and Doctor Watson to conceal yourselves among the stones, and if anything should happen there, you will be the first one on the scene."

Glancing over, I thought I saw a brief smile flash across my friend's face. Both he and I knew that Lestrade was playing to his vanity, and Holmes seemed quite content to appear obtuse to the Inspector's little charade.

"So, if my calculations are correct, we have a total of seven men to patrol some 28 square miles."

"Is Avebury that big?" I asked.

"Indeed," said Holmes. "I have been reading a great deal about these sites since the killings began, and perhaps a quote that may help put things in perspective for both you and Lestrade comes from the 17th-century antiquarian, John Aubrey, who wrote of Avebury, 'It does as much exceed in greatness the so renowned Stonehenge as a cathedral doeth a parish church.' Thus while the village is quite small, the stone circles and other prehistoric structures have been spread out over several miles. In fact, there is one theory put forth by a historian which opines that at one time, Avebury and Stonehenge may have been connected in some way.

113

"Now, as regards tonight, the one obvious benefit that we have is that the locale is sparsely populated. However, working against us is the scope of the area as well as the terrain. It's approximately a mile and a half from Avebury to Silbury Hill, and there is quite a distance between all four areas that you wish to patrol. In between, there are banks and ditches, and plenty of sheep grazing in the area.

"This will be a tremendous undertaking, Lestrade. I hope your men are up to the task."

"They will be, Mr. Holmes. They understand what is at stake. They all have police whistles, and we have devised a code whereby each officer, should he encounter anything suspicious, will blow his whistle a specified number of times to alert everyone else to his location." He then gave Homes and me whistles – "in case you should get separated" – and explained the code to us.

"That certainly sounds all well and good," said Holmes, "but let us hope the night passes quietly."

That said, Holmes and Lestrade continued to modify and refine the Inspector's plan all the way to Swindon. We then hired a carriage to drive the three of us to Avebury. During the drive, Holmes and Lestrade made small talk about fishing in the local streams.

It was just after dark when we finally arrived in Avebury. Leaving us at the Red Lion, where we had booked rooms for the night, Lestrade began to check on his men, who had concealed themselves near the various sites they had been assigned to watch. Returning nearly two hours later, he informed us that everyone was in place.

As we ate, Holmes told us of the Red Lion's history and the fact that it had claims to be the country's oldest inn, and he concluded with the fact that it was supposedly haunted by the wife of an innkeeper, who had caught her in the arms of another man and then killed them both.

"Her name was Florrie," said Holmes, "and perhaps you may catch a glimpse of her in your room before we leave."

As it was now fully dark outside, we left the Red Lion. We walked with Lestrade down between rows of stones as we made our way to The Sanctuary, yet another stone circle, and the West Kennet Long Barrow. Both are about a mile and a half from Avebury and they are separated from each other by about three-quarters of a mile.

We agreed to meet on the road in the morning, unless something brought us together sooner.

Holmes and I headed for the Long Barrow. As we walked, he gave me a brief description of the barrow that had been imparted to him by Professor Connors. "Scientists and antiquarians have been interested in this area for hundreds of years. In fact, the area was almost lost thanks to the ministrations of one Doctor Troope, an 18th-century charlatan who removed many bones from the burial chamber. He claimed that he used the bones to create a 'noble medicine' that worked wonders on many of his patients."

"How bizarre!" I exclaimed.

"The barrow itself is more than 300 feet long and one may enter into the burial chambers themselves. Unfortunately, the passage only extends about 40 feet, but one may still access four different chambers from it. I plan to conceal myself in the barrow,

115

Watson, and I should like you to set up a watch post from which you can see the entrance. If anyone should arrive, allow them to enter and then come to the stone with your weapon at the ready.

"Any questions, old friend?"

"No, but I must say this is one of the most unusual places that I have ever seen."

"Don't let your nerves get the better of you, Watson. Unless I miss my guess, nothing is going to happen."

"But what if we are set upon by a cult of crazed druids?" I protested.

"I can assure you that will not happen," said Holmes. "I believe that we are looking for a killer who is using the trappings of an ancient religion to conceal his acts."

"To what end?" I asked.

"When I have put all the pieces together, I assure you that you will be the first to know. Now, here we are. I'll conceal myself inside and you can look around for a suitable hiding place."

After leaving Holmes, I managed to find two large stones right near each other, and I concealed myself between them, in such a manner that I was terribly uncomfortable and thus far less likely to fall asleep.

I have spent many nights on watch with my friend, but knowing that a diabolical killer was preying on innocent young people helped me steel my resolve. Periodically, I would check my watch using the dark-lantern that I had brought with me. To say that time moved slowly that night, would be a gross understatement. Minutes seemed like hours and hours days, but finally I could see the sky just beginning to lighten when I heard four sharp blasts from a distant police whistle. Holmes had also heard them, for he emerged from the barrow and yelled "Silbury Hill, old friend."

Holmes and I then set off at a breakneck pace across the fields toward the mysterious mound. I later learned that Silbury Hill is the largest man-made mound in Europe and is roughly the size of the Egyptian Pyramid. As we ran, I heard the whistle blasts repeated a second and then a third time.

As we neared the hill, Holmes yelled back, "Hurry, Watson, I will need your assistance with this."

The four blasts were then sounded again. "Around the back," yelled Holmes, who was some 50 feet in front of me. I followed my friend, and I thought I heard Lestrade yelling in the distance as well.

Holmes began to ascend the hill, and I saw another figure standing quite close to the top. I heard Holmes yell to him, "Stay back! Don't touch anything!"

By the time I finally caught up with Holmes, I was quite winded and it took me a few minutes to catch my breath and compose myself. During that time, Lestrade and the other officers had arrived or were climbing the hill. Holmes turned to me and said, "Watson, keep everyone but Lestrade back at least 50 feet. And tell Lestrade to take a wide berth as he ascends the hill.

"After you have done that, join me by the body."

I descended some 50 feet back down the hill where I met Lestrade and passed along Holmes' instructions. He ordered his men to canvass the area looking for tracks of any kind, but to come no further up the hill until they were instructed to do so.

Lestrade and I then set out to our left and gradually ascended the hill until we were some 20 feet above the body. We then made our way back across until we were directly above Holmes, the constable and a figure prone on the grass.

As it had started to grow lighter, Holmes was on his knees examining the scene with his lens, He looked up and said, "Watson, please examine the body and tell me if anything significant strikes you."

As I approached the body, I could see that it was a woman, perhaps around 40. She was wearing a green dress that blended into the grass to a degree.

I heard the constable tell Lestrade, "I switched places a few times during the night. I only found her because as dawn was starting to break, I decided to conduct one more circuit of the entire hill about halfway up."

"Well done, Gribben," said Lestrade. "I can't believe that he has struck again, and this time right under our noses."

As I examined the body, I saw that she had been stabbed several times. The wounds were in various place, including her hands, which led me to believe that she had put up quite a struggle while trying to defend herself.

"Anything, Watson?"

"The wounds on the hands tell me she tried to fight off her attacker. Also, I am inclined to think given the pronounced rigor mortis that she was murdered at least 12 hours ago, perhaps longer."

"Excellent, Watson," said Holmes. Turning to Lestrade, he continued, "This is not the work of our 'deadly druid'."

"How can you can be so sure of that Mr. Holmes?" asked Lestrade. "She was killed on the druidic feast day, at a site that we had under consideration. Surely, this is the work of the same person."

"Where is the druidic symbol? The ogham writing? The branches placed around the body? No, Lestrade. It won't do. This is a crime committed by someone who would like us to think the druid killer has struck again."

"I'm still not convinced, Mr. Holmes. Perhaps, he spotted Gribben before he could administer his finishing touches."

"Perhaps, Lestrade. I will grant you that, but all the other victims also had one other thing in common."

"The puncture mark in the neck!" I exclaimed.

"Bravo, Watson, Have you found such a mark?"

"I looked for it and found none," I said.

"So then who killed this poor woman?" asked Lestrade.

"Give me time to examine the scene, and I may perhaps be able to provide you with an answer, or at least point you in the right direction."

Holmes then began a thorough examination of the poor woman's body. Fortunately, one of the constables had thought to bring a blanket, so we were able to cover her face after Holmes had finished.

He then began to examine the surrounding area, dropping to his stomach to examine particular spots and working his way slowly down to the base of the hill. This went on for some 20 minutes. When he had finished, he walked slowly back up, pausing to examine various spots in greater detail. After he had rejoined us, Lestrade began, "So what can you tell us, Mr. Holmes?"

"She was killed some distance away and then carried to this spot on the hill, so right away, we know that we are looking for a strong man in good physical condition. Climbing this hill is difficult enough, so doing it while carrying a body must be quite taxing, I imagine."

I could see Lestrade getting ready to interrupt, but I caught his eye and my friend continued uninterrupted.

"I would put his height at slightly above six feet, and he is right-handed. The angle of the wounds tell me his height, which is further substantiated by the footprints I found in the grass. There is one set of deeply indented marks ascending the hill and another set, far lighter, descending. The cuts on her dress and the lacerations on her skull all point to his being right-handed.

"I think he must be from somewhere around here, and I would wager that his face and neck might be very badly scratched. There are traces of skin under her fingernails. If I were pressed, I would say that the killer lives quite near or works with a forge. The cuffs of her dress contain very faint traces of coal dust from coke rather than bituminous coal. I should also think that he has very black hair that is just starting to show signs of grey. And finally, I believe that he considers himself a member of the upper-class and has quite the superior air."

"Mr. Holmes, I know far better than to doubt you, and I can follow all of the physical deductions you have made. I am assuming that you found a stray hair or two on the body for the color, but as for the upper class and the air of superiority, I must confess that I am baffled."

"Quite simple, Lestrade. Consider the dress. It is made of the finest brocade and the workmanship is flawless. Then look at her shoes, which are made of excellent leather. I do not think you will find too many servants attired in such finery. If we then take into account her jewelry, the wedding ring displays a certain craftsmanship as does the brooch she is wearing. They were costly, which certainly indicates a member of the upper class or one aspiring to be thought of as one.

"As for the superiority, he has lavished his attention and money on this woman, but now she is dead. I do not think this a crime of passion, but one that was obviously premeditated in that he tried to make it look like a druidic killing. To know that yesterday was a druidic feast would seem to indicate he is educated."

As the Inspector shook his head in bewilderment, Holmes said, "Come now, Lestrade, I have done everything but supply you with a photograph of him. Give the description to your men and have them canvass the surrounding towns. I do not think our man will be all that difficult to find."

Holmes and I watched as Lestrade summoned his men up the hill. After they had been gathered together, the Inspector related Holmes' description of the killer, He had hardly finished, when one of the constables said, "I saw just such a man in Marlborough yesterday, but his face wasn't scratched."

"Did you now?" asked Lestrade.

"Yes sir. I hired my horse from him."

"A stable hand?" asked Lestrade, casting a wry look at Holmes.

"No sir. He owned the stable and the blacksmith shop. While we were talking, he told me that he had been a farrier in his youth, but he had spent several years in South Africa from which he had returned a rich man."

"And did you get this fellow's name?" asked Lestrade.

"Yes sir," replied the constable. "He said his name was Henry Dalton."

"Well, why don't we pay a visit to Mr. Dalton before we head back to London?" Lestrade asked. "You have to return the horse anyway."

Lestrade then pulled Holmes aside and said, "I hope you are right about this Mr. Holmes. A quick arrest would go a long way toward lengthening my career."

"If you find things as I told you," said Holmes, "I believe that you may able to arrest Mr. Dalton with impunity. However, his incarceration advances our other case not a whit."

"Well, let us clear this matter up, and then we can redouble our efforts as we have almost seven weeks before the winter solstice."

We then took our leave from Lestrade, checked out of the inn and hired a carriage to take us to Swindon. Holmes was unusually quiet during the trip. He continued his silence aboard the train, and it was only as we neared London that he finally spoke, announcing, "And so it is settled, Watson."

"What is?" I asked, being totally baffled.

"I must attempt the impossible and divine the future in order to prevent a crime before it even occurs."

Chapter 16

The next afternoon Lestrade called upon us at Baker Street.

"And how did Mr. Dalton respond to the charges?" asked Holmes.

"Oh, he denied them at first. Claimed that he and his wife had had a terrible row, and that she had taken one of his carriages and driven off.

"But when I saw the scratches on his face, and the dark hair going grey at the temples, I knew he was our man. It took a few hours of interrogation, but eventually he broke down and confessed. It seems his wife had an eye for the gentlemen, and he had actually followed her halfway to Avebury where she was going to meet a gentleman before confronting her.

"He said that she laughed at him, called him an old fool and said he didn't know how to keep a wife. I think it was her sharp tongue that got the better of him. He admits that he was in a blind rage and the next thing he knew, she was dead."

"And you believe him?" asked Holmes.

"Why would he lie after admitting to murdering her?"

"Because juries are far more apt to forgive a crime of passion than they are premeditated murder, especially if the wronged party committed the crime. However, this is a case of cold-blooded murder. How convenient that they had a row on a druidic feast day! How convenient that he left her body halfway up the hill at Avebury, a druidic site! No, Lestrade. If you want to see justice served, then I fear you must insist that Mr. Dalton tell you the truth about his relationship with his wife."

"Well, I will certainly consider that," said the Inspector. "Now, the next date we must concern ourselves with is the winter solstice, is it not Mr. Holmes?"

"Indeed," said Holmes, "in druidic lore the winter solstice is often called the Alban Arthur, which Professor Connors informs me can be translated as 'The Light of Arthur'."

"Not King Arthur?" exclaimed Lestrade.

"That depends on which group of druids you choose to follow," said Holmes. "There are those who believe that on that day, King Arthur is reborn as the Sun Child. After all, once the solstice has passed the days start to grow longer."

"And the other druids? The ones who don't believe in King Arthur?" I asked.

"They see the light as belonging to the constellation Ursa Major, the Great Bear, also sometimes referred to as the Plough. Arthur or Art is the Gaelic word for 'bear'."

"Mr. Holmes, this just gets more confusing. Every time I think we are taking a step forward, there's another new element introduced. Will it never end?"

"Lestrade, I think the confusion is deliberate. If you had planned a series of crimes, wouldn't you do everything possible to throw your pursuers off the scent?"

Before Lestrade could reply, Holmes answered his own question: "Of course you would. So, these are merely red herrings designed to make us stray from the path that we should follow."

"You sound as though you know who killed these people," said Lestrade.

"I have a suspect, Lestrade. The problem is there is at least one other involved."

"Tell me whom you suspect, and I'll invite them to the Yard for a nice long conversation," said the Inspector.

"I should very much like to, Inspector, but I am afraid that's not possible at this time."

"Why do you say that?" asked Lestrade.

"These are some very intelligent people that we are dealing with Lestrade. Were you to bring them down to the Yard, I can assure you that they would confess to nothing."

"How can you be so sure of that?"

"Because they have been very careful. Their planning has been meticulous. They know that they have left no clues behind. Were you to make them aware that they are under suspicion, they might cease their activities altogether, and then where would we be? No, Lestrade, for the moment they must be allowed to proceed unencumbered.

"I think they have one final crime planned, and then the killings will cease. So our only chance to apprehend them is to catch them in the act."

"And can we do that?" asked the Inspector incredulously.

"I believe that we can. Consider this: We know approximately when the next murder will take place – on or about the winter solstice. I have a developed a theory as to where the crime will take place. I believe that I even have ascertained the identity of the person behind the plot. Were we hard-pressed, we could move now. However, the case we would be forced to present is a tenuous one, built largely on conjecture and circumstantial evidence; moreover, I want to apprehend everyone who had a hand in this, and that is why I counsel caution."

I could see that Lestrade was less than pleased with Holmes' deductions, but there was certainly no arguing with the logic of them on the surface. After he had considered them for a moment or two, he spoke, "I don't like it, Mr. Holmes."

"Neither do I, Lestrade. If someone else should die, I shall never forgive myself, but I am convinced that to move against them now is to hazard all when we need not. Our best strategy is to lull the killers into a false sense of security. We have seven weeks to plan, and for the first time, the playing field is not totally tipped in their direction."

"I will be guided by you, Mr. Holmes."

"You know, Lestrade, if the press were to learn that Mr. Dalton had been apprehended for the murder of his wife, who died in a manner similar to the other druid victims, well, there's just no telling what conclusions they might jump to."

"That's a capital idea, Mr. Holmes. Perhaps if they believe the police are no longer looking for them, they will be a little less careful."

I saw a slight smile cross my old friend's face, and I could tell that he was going to allow Lestrade to enjoy his moment in the limelight.

"Brilliant, Inspector. Remember though, just as before, no details about the branches or the ogham. Just let them know that the murder was committed in a like manner and that all indications point to the suspect you have in custody."

"Well that will certainly keep my superiors from breathing down my neck," said Lestrade. "However," he continued, "catching them before their next atrocity now becomes more important than ever. If the Yard were to come out of this looking foolish, well I don't have to tell you what might happen."

Lestrade left soon after, a decidedly happier man than when he had arrived.

After he had departed, I said to Holmes, "Do you feel any regret about saddling Mr. Dalton with three murders that he didn't commit?"

"None," replied my friend. "I don't know why Dalton killed his wife, but I suspect that were we to investigate, we might discover that he was the philanderer – not she. At any rate, he took an innocent life, and he must pay for his crime. If we can use his guilt to prevent another killing, it seems that's some small atonement for his heinous act."

I considered informing Holmes that atoning for one's sins is normally a matter of conscience and usually done voluntarily, but I decided against it.

The next day the papers were filled with stories about the 'Druid of Death' being captured. On my way to my club, I must have passed at least six different newsboys all hawking their papers, yelling, "Deadly Druid in custody" or some variation thereof.

When I returned home that afternoon, I found Holmes perusing his copy of "The Origin of Tree Worship."

"Anything of interest?" I asked.

"Just double-checking a few conclusions," he replied.

"About trees?"

"The trees are the key to this case," replied Holmes.

"Really?"

"Of course, all along this has been an exercise in misdirection. The tree branches stand at the center of everything.

Consider, they are the only things that had to be brought to the crime scenes. In a sense, they are the only foreign objects to be found; now, the more we know about the trees and their locations in the countryside, the closer we are to solving the case. There are no trees at Stonehenge, as you know. Nor are there trees at the Uffington White Horse or Drizzlecombe."

"True enough," I said, "but trees grow everywhere."

"Yes," replied Holmes, "but not all trees can be found in all places. Some can be found only in very specific locales." Pausing, he looked at me and with a mischievous grin added, "And some trees really don't belong here at all, but that remains to be seen I suppose."

Since I could get nothing further from Holmes, I contented myself with a thought that has often crossed my mind, "The man can be absolutely maddening."

As the weeks passed, I saw less and less of Holmes. He would be gone for a just a few hours, and at other times, he would disappear for three or four days at a stretch. I noticed that as we moved toward the end of November, his absences grew longer. I could only assume that he was exploring avenues of inquiry with regard to the case. I also believed that he was doing everything possible to prevent another killing.

When he was at home, he barely ate, choosing to immerse himself in a number of different tomes on an array of subjects and studying maps that detailed different parts of the kingdom.

One afternoon, I walked in and found him poring over a large map that he had spread out on the floor. I recognized it as the map that Professor Connors had made for him shortly before the summer solstice murder. "Still following the same trail?" I asked.

"I see no reason to leave a trail that has not led me astray."

"But it hasn't led you to the killer either," I offered.

"True enough. Although the locations of the first three murders can be seen on the map," he said pointing to different spots, "as well as the death of the unfortunate Mrs. Dalton, I do not think this is the key to the next murder."

"I must admit that I am lost."

"You remember the winter solstice has very strong connections to the Arthurian legend?"

"Yes," I replied. "What of it?"

"Originally, I was inclined to believe the next killing might well take place in or around Glastonbury, the location believed to be the burial site of King Arthur."

"And of Queen Guinevere as well," I added.

"Only if you believe the most romantic of the legends, something I am disinclined to do. No, the whole Mordred, Lancelot, Round Table nonsense came later and was added incrementally by an array of different authors from Geoffrey of Monmouth to Chretian de Troyes to Sir Thomas Malory. All flights of fancy," he exclaimed.

"So if that's not the connection, then what is?"

"Think. I've just listed several of the main figures, but whom have I omitted?"

"Not Gawain?" I asked. "This isn't tied to that Green Knight story, is it?"

"No," Holmes said, "though I suppose the Yuletide connection and the pagan symbolism might lead one in that direction."

"I give up," I sputtered.

"The original druid, perhaps?"

"Merlin!" I exclaimed.

"Exactly," I was hoping to find a stone circle near Glastonbury, but according to Connors' map, one doesn't exist. Which then leads me to conclude that our killer is quite literally going back to the beginning. Consider that Merlin first appears in Geoffrey's *Historia Regum Britanniae,* written around 1130. However, Geoffrey based his wizard on the figures of Merlinus Caledonensis, a North Brythonic prophet and madman with absolutely no connection to the legendary Arthur; and Ambrosius Aurelianus, a Roman-British chieftain. Together, the two figures were joined to form Merlin Ambrosius. The problem for me is that, according to most legends, Merlin is reportedly buried in the Broceliande Forest in Brittany."

"Why is that a problem?"

"Thus far, all of the killings have taken place here in England. Since I suspect that the whole druid motif is little more than an elaborate diversion, smoke and mirrors if you will, I cannot see them journeying to France to complete the illusion. As a result, I have been searching for possible sites that fit their leitmotif and would allow them to continue and complete the illusion, but are closer to home."

"Why must they complete the illusion?"

"Surely, that is obvious," he replied.

"Not to me. First, I didn't know there was an illusion until you just said so. Second, why must they complete it?"

"Should they stop, the druidic aspects of the killings will come under much closer scrutiny as will the killings themselves, and that is something they are desperate to avoid."

"If they are so 'desperate,' how can you be so sure they won't go to France?"

"Too easy to trace. Their absence here would be conspicuous, especially with Christmas so close, and their presence in France when another killing took place might just provide us with enough circumstantial evidence to sway a jury. No, Watson, they will strike one last time, and then they will cease and perhaps disappear, and that is why it is imperative that we apprehend them before they do."

"You talk about circumstantial evidence, yet right now, you have no evidence at all to present to a jury, do you?"

"Well played, Watson. You are quite right. At present, I have no hard evidence but I will certainly gather a sufficient quantity before I even suggest that Lestrade bring charges. These are killers who must not be allowed to go free over a point of law.

"I have charted my course, Watson. And I will stay the course and see justice done."

While Holmes is normally quite reserved, he had grown increasingly passionate as he spoke. When he looked at me with those piercing gray eyes, I could tell that on this matter, he was not a man to be trifled with.

Chapter 17

"I do believe that we are in the clear," he exclaimed one afternoon as she sat reading in the library.

"What on Earth are you talking about?"

Holding up a newspaper, he said, "The police have arrested a man from Marlborough in connection with the killing on Silbury Hill."

"From Marlborough?"

"Yes, of all places! His name is Henry Dalton and he murdered his wife in much the same manner that the other killings took place."

"When you say 'in much the same manner,' what exactly do you mean?" she asked.

"The body was found about halfway up Silbury Hill, an historic site. She was killed on the night of October 31st, the feast of Samhain. She was stabbed to death, and the police are looking to charge him with the other murders as well."

"Was there a druidic symbol on her forehead? Ogham writing on the body? Had it been surrounded by tree branches?"

"The papers do not mention any of those things."

"Nor have they since we put this plan into motion, and the silence on those details speaks volumes. They have withheld those facts deliberately."

"Why would they do that?"

"Isn't it obvious? They have made little progress on the case, and they were wary enough to anticipate someone emulating our style."

"But, in this case, couldn't they have interrupted him before he finished?"

"I suppose that is possible although highly unlikely. Even if they had caught him in the act, they have merely to ask him what the symbols mean or to translate the ogham. Obviously, he will refuse, but I believe this to be a very clever ploy by the police in an effort to get us to lower our guard."

"So, you think we must still continue with the plan."

"I see no other alternative," she replied. "We want the police as distracted and as busy as possible. The more murders they have to solve, the better for us."

"So long as we don't get caught."

She said to him, "Given everything that is at stake, I never expected to hear such moral quibbling from you of all people. Perhaps I might have been better served by a different partner."

However, the seeds of doubt had been sown. "I must keep a much closer eye on him in the future and bolster him at every turn," she resolved. Then in an attempt to break the tension, she asked, "Is there any mention in the paper of Sherlock Holmes?"

"No," he answered. "I read the story twice."

"Now that I find odd. We know that Holmes is involved, yet there is no mention made of it."

"Perhaps the papers are deliberately withholding that information as well," he offered.

"I am certain you are correct," she said. "However, I have the feeling that it might benefit us greatly were we able to find Holmes something else to focus on – at least for the near future."

"Have you any ideas?"

"I have two possibilities, but they are both just rough plans. They will need to be refined and perfected before we can even consider employing one, or possibly both, of them."

"Would you care to tell me about them?"

Although she really had no interest in discussing her plans with him, she decided to share her thoughts. After all, they were in this together – at least for the moment and hopefully forever. Better to assuage any doubts he might have at the present, she thought, than to have him question her at some crucial moment in the future.

So for the next 15 minutes, she discussed her ideas. When she had finished, he looked at her and said, "Brilliant. I always knew you were a scheming woman, but now it is obvious that your devious nature knows no bounds. I particularly like the second idea."

"I am so glad that you approve, she said, all the while thinking, "I wonder what your reaction would be, were I to tell you the third plan that I am developing."

Interrupting her thought, he asked, "How soon do you think it will be before we can begin?"

"That's one of the details I am working on," she answered, "but no more of this for now. Let us take another look at the map and begin to plan our grand finale."

Chapter 18

On the first of December, Professor Connors arrived at Baker Street late in the afternoon. After Mrs. Hudson had shown him in, he said, "I have some important news for Mr. Holmes."

As Holmes had stepped out and I had no idea when he would return, I informed the professor that he was welcome to wait if his schedule permitted. He seemed amenable to the idea so we passed a pleasant hour discussing subjects, ranging from the construction of the stone circles to the possible religious connotations they carried. As he digressed into the differences between the Paleolithic and Neolithic periods, he must have seen the look of confusion of my face.

"I do apologize, Doctor Watson. Those terms are fairly new, and they may not have made their way into the popular lexicon just yet. In fact, they are less than 40 years old, and I suppose they largely remain the province of the scientific community."

"Are they?" I asked.

"Indeed," he replied. "The term 'palaeolithic' was coined by the archaeologist John Lubbock in 1865. It derives from Greek: *palaios* or 'old' and *lithos* or 'stone'. Quite literally it is translated as the 'old age of the stone' or 'Old Stone Age'."

He continued to wax poetic about the Neolithic period as well, all the while I wanted only to hear what news he had for Holmes.

He was so earnest and scholarly that I hadn't the heart to tell him that all his information was grist for Holmes' mill and not mine. Fortunately, it was only a minute or two later that Holmes came through the door.

"Professor Connors," he said, "what a pleasant surprise it is to see you. I hope you haven't been waiting long."

"Not at all," Connors replied, "and Doctor Watson here is an excellent listener."

"I can certainly vouch for that," said Holmes. "On many occasions, he has proven himself quite useful as a sounding board, who occasionally takes issues with the points I raise. However, you didn't come here to talk about Watson. How may I be of service Professor?"

"I believe that I may be of service to you, Mr. Holmes."

"I'm a tad confused here," said my friend.

"Remember a few weeks back, you asked me to look into the various burial places of Merlin?"

"Yes, and you said that according to most legends he is entombed somewhere in Brittany."

"I did say that, but now I'm going to utter just one word, and see if you can figure it out."

"And the word?" asked Holmes.

"Marlborough," replied Connors.

As Holmes pondered Connors' pronouncement, I couldn't tell whether he was angry or overjoyed.

Eventually, he smiled a rather wan smile. "Of course," he said, "I have been looking for the exotic, the *outre*, if you will. And the whole time, the key has been staring me in the face.

"Oh, I have been a blind beetle, Watson."

"Well, I am still in the dark," I said. "Would either of you care to explain what is going on?"

Holmes looked at Connors and said "I will defer to your expertise."

Connors smiled and quickly warmed to his subject. "When Mr. Holmes told me that the burial place of Merlin might play a role in this case, I immediately thought of Merlin Sylvestris, who was said to have been baptized and converted to Christianity by Saint Kentigern on the altar stone at Drumelzier, a village on the Scottish borders.

"According to legend, Merlin prophesized his own death of falling, drowning and stabbing and, in fact, died his three deaths there after he was chased off a cliff by shepherds where he tripped and fell, impaled himself upon a fishing rod on the sea bed and died with his head under the water.

"In fact, there is a prophecy that states:

'When Tweed and Powsail meet at Merlin's grave,

Scotland and England shall one monarch have.'

"If you believe in legends, that prophecy came to fruition in 1603 when Queen Elizabeth I died childless and without any immediate heirs. As a result, her second cousin, King James VI of Scotland, was made monarch of both countries. Allegedly, on the day of the Union of Crowns the Tweed is said to have burst its banks and its waters mingled with those of Powsail Burn at the site of Merlin's grave."

"Stuff and nonsense," I exclaimed.

"Perhaps," replied Connors evenly, "it's too bad that we shall never know the veracity of the legend. At any rate, as there are certain similarities between the area and the other sites, I decided to continue my research and see if I might find something more similar to the other scenes. Also, the presence of Saint

Kentigern, a sixth-century holy man in the legend seemed to preclude that location as it put the events in the wrong time period.

"As I mentioned, a second legend, perhaps the most popular of them all, has the wizard buried in Normandy and there are certainly plenty of stone circles in the region, but the fact that all the crimes have taken place in England gave me pause.

"It was an offhand remark by a colleague, Jane Dieulafoy, a Frenchwoman noted primarily for her work in Iran that jarred my memory and made me recall a trip I had taken as a youngster to Marlborough. I spent much of the day running up and down Merlin's Mound and playing hide-and-seek."

"Merlin's Mound!" I exclaimed, "Never heard of it."

Holmes looked at Connors and said, "May I, Professor?" After Connors had nodded, Holmes took up the narrative. "As you know Watson, Marlborough is quite close to both Avebury and Stonehenge. That alone would make a point of interest for us.

"The mound itself is located on the grounds of Marlborough College, I believe. Having spent a day or two there in my youth, I am somewhat familiar with it, but for some reason, it escaped my memory, perhaps because I only ever heard it referred to as the Marlborough Mound.

"At any rate, it is a rather bizarre conical mound of earth with a path that spirals around from top to bottom, giving it a sort of terraced appearance. Like Silbury Hill, it is a man-made mound, and there is quite of lot of history surrounding the location, I believe.

"However, what makes this hill different from the others we have looked at is the fact that there is an abundance of trees growing on all sides. Trees, Watson!"

I can assure you that Holmes' reference was not lost on me. At that point, Connors said, "Mr. Holmes, if I may add something." After Holmes nodded, he continued, "According to many myths, Merlin built the circle at Stonehenge, and while I do not ascribe to that rather fanciful school of thought, I find myself in agreement with any number of other scholars who hold that the sarsen stones of the largest circle at Stonehenge came from the Marlborough Downs."

Holmes clapped his hands, "And there you have it. The circle has been closed."

"One more point, Mr. Holmes," said Connors. "Again, this is only one school of thought, but there are those who believe that the town Marlborough may be a derivation of the phrase 'Merlin's Barrow.' In fact, the town's motto is *Ubi nunc sapientis ossa Merlini*. (Where now are the bones of wise Merlin?) And while it certainly makes for a good story, I am inclined to believe the town name is actually derived from the medieval term for chalky ground 'marl,' which thus translates to the 'town on chalk'."

"Professor Connors, you have done splendidly," enthused Holmes. "I cannot thank you enough for all your help."

"I just hope you catch the fiend responsible for these atrocities," said Connors.

After a bit more small talk, and another offer from Connors to call upon him should we need further assistance, he went on his way.

"Slowly but surely, Watson, all the pieces are coming together. In addition to when the next crime will be committed, I now know where."

"I assume you think the next crime will take place at this Merlin's Mound."

"Were I a wagering man, such as yourself, I should be inclined to bet on it."

"Don't you think the killer is taking a tremendous risk?"

"The killer takes a chance every time he strikes, but what makes this a greater risk?"

"You said the mound is located on the grounds of Marlborough College."

"And so it is."

"Well, there are always students about at all hours of the day and night. Who knows who might be out and about that night?"

"The winter solstice falls on Friday, December 22nd. With Christmas falling on that Monday, I am inclined to think that the grounds will be deserted. The students will have left to spend the holidays with their families. If there are classes on that Friday, they will be dismissed long before midnight arrives. No, Watson, that's the genius of this locale. It completes the illusion, and were we not involved, the local constabulary and the Yard could spend years looking for a secret pagan society that never existed to begin with."

"And since you now know the date and the place, do you know the killer as well?"

"I believe that I have definitely identified one of the guilty parties," my friend said, "but at present, the other still eludes me. However, I intend to close the net so tightly that there is no chance of his escape."

We continued our discussion through dinner, and then there was a gentle knock on the door.

"Come in Mrs. Hudson," said Holmes.

Our landlady entered carrying a telegram. "I am sorry to disturb you Mr. Holmes, but this just arrived by messenger. I was told that a reply is expected, and the messenger is waiting downstairs."

"What in the world?" I exclaimed.

"There is only one way to find out," said Holmes, tearing open the envelope. He read the telegram and then looked at me and said, "Lady Deveron would like to meet with me tomorrow."

Sitting at his desk, Holmes jotted a quick note. Turning to Mrs. Hudson, he said, "Give this to boy." Reaching into his pocket, he pulled out a few coins and said, "Give these to the lad as well. And Mrs. Hudson, thank you very much."

"What could Her Ladyship possibly want with you?" I asked.

"I suppose we shall have to wait until tomorrow to find out," replied Holmes. "She said that she would like to call upon us at one o'clock, if it is convenient. In my reply, I put myself at Her Ladyship's disposal."

When I awoke the next morning, I entered our rooms to find Holmes in conversation with Wiggins, a young street Arab and the de facto leader of Holmes' so-called "Baker Street Irregulars."

"How you handle it is up to you," Holmes told the boy.

"Righto, guv'nor."

Holmes then gave the boy some coins, and said, "There's double that if you are able to find out what I want to know."

After the lad had departed, I looked at Holmes and said, "Pray tell what was that all about?"

"A minor matter," replied my friend, "Nothing that you need concern yourself with."

"Have you told Mrs. Hudson that you are expecting a visitor?"

"I have, and she insisted upon baking some fresh scones just in case Her Ladyship should desire a light repast with her tea."

"Do you know that she will take tea?"

"No, but when I raised that exact point with Mrs. Hudson, she grew adamant. Rather than argue, I acquiesced."

"You are learning, Holmes."

The minutes crept by and at exactly one, a large Clarence pulled by four grand horses arrived in front of our lodgings, and Lady Judith Deveron emerged from the curtained carriage. A few minutes later, there was a knock on the door and Holmes rose to answer it."

"Your Ladyship," he said bowing slightly, "I trust you had a pleasant journey."

"It was tolerable," she replied, "but I didn't come here to discuss the shortcomings of the British rail system, Mr. Holmes."

Showing her to a seat, Holmes then pulled up a chair opposite her. He then said, "I see you are a very direct woman. How may I be of service?"

At that point, Mrs. Hudson knocked on the door and entered the room with a tray bearing tea and the freshly baked scones. She curtseyed to Lady Deveron and said, "I baked these fresh for you."

After she had departed, Lady Deveron said, "I don't think I can eat anything."

"You must keep your strength up," I admonished her, "and Mrs. Hudson's scones are a rare treat indeed."

She then took a single scone, and agreed to a cup of tea with just lemon.

"And now back to business," said Holmes.

Her Ladyship started to speak and then gazed at me and then back a Holmes. "I assure you, Your Ladyship, that Dr. Watson is the very soul of discretion. Feel free to speak your mind."

"Mr. Holmes, I read about that man Dalton, they arrested. Did he kill my son?"

"The papers believe that he did," Holmes replied.

"And what do you believe?"

"I believe that the person or persons responsible for the murder of Lord Deveron may still be at large."

"I knew it," she said almost in a whisper.

"Will the police catch these people?" she asked.

"I possess some small degree of talent," said Holmes, "but divining the future is one skill that I have not yet mastered."

She looked at Holmes for a second and then said, "As you might expect, thus far I have found the police lacking."

When neither of us responded, she continued, "May I ask your opinion Mr. Holmes?"

"By all means."

"Do you think if I offered a reward for information it might help?"

"Well, it certainly couldn't hurt," replied Holmes evenly. "In my experience, honor among thieves is more myth than reality."

"Then I shall do it," she replied. "I cannot continue without seeing justice done for Trent. Shall we say 5,000 pounds?"

"My word," I exclaimed. "That is most generous."

"You have seen my estate, Dr. Watson. Without Trent, I am all alone. If my money can do some good then so be it." Turning to Holmes, she said, "Mr. Holmes, will you handle the arrangements? I will be more than happy to reimburse you for your time."

"Under ordinary circumstances, I would be more than happy to assist Your Ladyship; unfortunately, I find myself overwhelmed at the present time. Between us, I am currently assisting one of the leading houses of Europe in a matter that requires the utmost delicacy."

To say that Her Ladyship looked crestfallen would not even begin to capture the depths of disappointment that coursed across her face.

Seeing this, Holmes said, "However, here is what we can do. Arrange the details of the reward with your solicitor. Have all responses sent to him, and he can then forward them to Dr. Watson. Although I cannot give it my full attention at this time, I will devote whatever spare time I have to examining the replies after Doctor Watson has culled the wheat from the chaff.

"I do not know if this endeavor will bear fruit, Your Ladyship. But I certainly applaud you for trying."

"Thank you, Mr. Holmes. I will do exactly as you suggested." Then she turned to me and I could feel for the woman's loss. "And thank you, Dr. Watson. I do not know how I shall ever be able to repay you."

"If justice is done, that is reward enough."

"I shall go to my solicitor immediately."

"Excellent," said Holmes. "Dr. Watson will see you out."

As I walked Lady Deveron to the door, Holmes disappeared into his bedroom. He returned a minute later and watched Lady Deveron as she walked around her carriage and entered it from the other side. The Clarence then clattered down the street. He continued to look out the window for another moment or two and then nodded.

After he had returned to his chair, I said, "Well thank you for that, Mr. Holmes."

"Come now, Watson, had I not conscripted you, I have no doubt that you would have volunteered to help a damsel in distress."

"Be that as it may, Holmes. It was still a bit cheeky on your part. And what new case have you undertaken that would draw you away from the druid killings, especially as the 22nd is less than three weeks away."

"One that requires absolute secrecy. Although I cannot share the details with you at the present, I promise it will make quite an addition to your chronicles if I am able to complete it successfully.

"As a result, I expect to leave for the Continent for a few days starting tomorrow, but I swear to return well before the 22nd. Although I cannot leave you my itinerary, I promise that I shall stay in close contact with you. Remember, Watson, I am counting on you to separate the wheat from the chaff."

Chapter 19

Holmes was as good as his word. When I called for breakfast the next morning, Mrs. Hudson informed me that my friend had once again arisen early, telling her that he hoped to be back within the week.

He had also left me a note. As I ate my breakfast, I read its contents:

Dear Watson,

> After all that we have been through together, how I wish you could accompany me. However, as I indicated, this is a matter of extreme delicacy. I am counting on you to eliminate all the false leads that may arise from Lady Deveron's most generous offer. I am hopeful that her reward may result in at least one or two pieces of useful information. As these are dangerous foes, please do not take any action until I return.

> I remain your loyal comrade-in-arms,

> S.H.

I could not remain angry with my friend, and I was determined to do my best to separate "the wheat from the chaff" for him.

To that end, I sent out for all the morning papers. As you might expect, Lady Deveron's offer of a reward had attracted a great deal of attention. As I read the various stories, retelling the murder of young Lord Deveron, I wondered how long it would be before I would hear from her solicitor, a Charles Wells, Esq.

I spent most of the day taking care of some financial affairs at my bank and lunching at my club. When I returned home, there was an envelope waiting for me. It had been messengered over from Mr. Wells.

He too had written a brief note.

Dear Dr. Watson,

> I have no idea what to make of these. I hope you can make some sense out of them.

> Sincerely,

> Charles J. Wells, Esq.

There were five notes addressed to Wells in the envelope. Two proposed that the killer was Jack the Ripper returned from his long hiatus while two others suggested that the killings were the first steps in the return of the druids to dominance.

The fourth note, cryptic in the extreme, quoted the Bible. It took me a few minutes to find the verse, but since I had heard it before, my memory served me well. It was a quote from the Book of Revelations that read:

> "And I looked, and behold
> a pale horse: and his name
> that sat on him was Death,
> and Hell followed with him.

And power was given unto them over the <u>fourth</u> part of the earth, to kill with sword, and with hunger, and with death, and with the beasts of the earth."

The letter had been neatly printed on cheap paper. I knew that Holmes could make more of it than I had. Although I must admit that while it said nothing on the surface that appeared to relate to this case, the reference to a "pale horse" seemed to harken back to the White Horse of Uffington. The fact that the word "fourth" had been underlined also seemed to me to portend something ominous as the next would be the fourth murder. After I had placed the first four in one large envelope, I kept that one separate, assigning it to its own envelope.

Every day thereafter at exactly four o'clock an envelope would arrive via messenger at our lodgings. Most days there were one or two missives inside. Occasionally, it contained a brief note from the solicitor that read simply, "Nothing today."

This went on for approximately one week, and the only other "wheat" that I could separate was a note that read, "Beware the coming of the wicker man."

I knew from my own research as well as what Holmes had told me that Caesar had written of the druids performing human sacrifices by constructing a giant man of wicker and imprisoning their victims within the structure before setting it on fire.

I could not take it seriously, but since it indirectly referenced a druidic practice, I assigned it to the second envelope which now had two kernels of "wheat" for Holmes to consider.

On December 5th, I received a wire from Holmes that read simply, "Things proceed apace. Expect to return within the week. S.H."

My friend proved true to his word, for on the evening of Dec. 10th, shortly before dinner time, I heard his familiar tread on the stairs, and shortly after the door was thrown wide as Holmes entered our sitting room.

After removing his coat and hat, he threw himself into his chair and announced, "Watson, it is so good to be home. I cannot tell you how glad I am to see you again."

"Your case on the Continent. I assume it went well?"

"About as well as could be expected," he replied rather ambiguously. "And have you been hearing from Mr. Wells?"

"He has been most officious," I replied and I then detailed for Holmes the events that had transpired, holding back my two grains of "wheat" until the end. "And now, if you have time, you may want to look at these two notes."

"Only two attracted your attention?" asked Holmes. "I had rather expected more given the size of the reward."

"As had I, but I think you will agree that these two may bear further investigation."

Holmes took the notes from me, and after reading the first said, "So now we have moved from druids to Christianity. The 'pale horse' reference is intriguing, I grant you that and the references to Death and Hell and the word fourth being underlined are certainly suggestive."

"What do you make of them?"

After he had read the second, he took out his lens and examined both quite carefully. As he conducted his examination, he would occasionally mutter a comment – "The paper tells us nothing" – before returning to the missives. After he had finished, he sat in his chair in silence and proceeded to light his pipe.

After a few minutes, I was unable to contain myself. "Well?"

"Oh, I do apologize, Watson. Although he has tried to disguise his writing, they were quite obviously penned by the same person. See the rather distinctive crosses on the 't's. Also notice the overly pointed 'w's. Although there are only two 'w's in the second letter, they are virtually identical to those in the first.

"Also, notice that neither references the reward. Rather an oddity don't you think, since the letters were sent to Lady Deveron's solicitor in response to her advertisement of said reward."

"So then what is the purpose?"

"I think these letters are intended to distract us. They are designed to make us think the killer may return to Uffington or perhaps to have us scour the countryside in hopes of discovering the site of an ancient wicker man."

"Why would you say that?"

"Bear with me a moment, Watson," said Holmes, as he pulled a piece of paper from his jacket pocket. Unfolding it, he placed it beside the other two letters and began to examine all three.

"Why would I say that? Because I believe that the same person who sent us the letter written in ogham is also the author of your two kernels of wheat."

"This grows increasingly bizarre!"

"You think so," remarked Holmes. "I would beg to differ. I think the case grows increasingly clearer. All we need now is to put our hands on the killer."

"So then you know who it is?"

"At the moment, I fear that I cannot provide you with the name he is using," replied Holmes, "but I believe that I can identify his employer. I have no idea exactly how this will work itself out – yet. However, I can promise you one thing: Justice will be served."

Chapter 20

The next two weeks were filled with Holmes coming and going at all hours. He also met with Lestrade on several occasions in our lodgings. Unfortunately, as I was covering for another colleague who was on his honeymoon, I missed many of those planning sessions. When I would press Holmes for details, he would simply respond, "All in due time; all in due time."

Finally, on December 14th, just after we had finished lunch, Lestrade arrived. After he had settled himself, he looked at Holmes and said, "Mr. Holmes, I have done everything that you asked. My future at the Yard is entirely in your hands."

Holmes looked at Lestrade, and for a moment, I thought I detected a brief show of emotion of my friend's face. If I did, it passed quickly as Holmes lit his pipe and then said to Lestrade, "I can assure you Inspector that you have a long and distinguished career in front of you, and bringing this killer to justice may well be its apex."

"I do hope you are right, Mr. Holmes."

"How many men have you secured for our little expedition?"

"I recruited five, just as you instructed. Together, with yourself, Dr. Watson and me that makes eight."

"Excellent, Lestrade. Has any of them left yet?"

"Two have already arrived at the village; another is leaving tonight, and the other two are ready to depart tomorrow."

"So by the time the 22nd arrives, they will have insinuated themselves into the pattern of daily life there to varying degrees," said Holmes.

"As much as they are able," replied Lestrade. "We did get rather lucky in that one of the lads had a friend in the village and asked if he might impose upon him for the holidays. He sold him quite a tale of woe, and from what I can gather will be welcomed with open arms."

"I don't think things could have gone much more smoothly," replied Holmes.

"Nor I, Mr. Holmes."

"Let us then meet again on Monday," said Holmes. "Your men have orders to report daily?"

"I am to receive one report each evening that will encompass the progress of all five. They were instructed to send the wires discreetly. We have worked out a rather crude code. They were also told not to use the village post office, but to make their way to a neighboring village to send the wires."

"You have outdone yourself, Lestrade. I don't believe that you have missed a trick."

The Inspector positively beamed at Holmes' compliment, and responded with a simple, "I'm just doing my job, Mr. Holmes."

After he had left, I said, "That was quite nice of you to bolster Lestrade's spirits with your words."

"He has done his best," replied Holmes. "I should have proceeded quite differently, and I will if I must. However, I do understand the restraints that confine Lestrade's actions and all too often dictate his choices."

"My word, Holmes."

"Come now, Watson. We have been toiling on this case for nearly nine months – nine months. Surely, a little prevarication on

154

my part in the interest of maintaining morale is understandable. Lestrade has done nothing wrong. I'm just hoping that we can depend on his men. After all, I merely confided to you that his course of action and mine would have been quite different."

"I understand. Perhaps the strain is starting to wear on me as well."

"Watson, you have been the one fixed point throughout this whole sordid affair. I promise you, my friend, it will soon be over."

At that moment, Mrs. Hudson knocked on the door and announced, "Your envelope is here, Dr. Watson."

"I wonder what old Wells has sent our way today," I remarked.

Upon opening the envelope, I discovered that it contained three pieces of paper. The first one maintained the murders were the work of a group of anarchists living in the East End. The second ascribed the crimes to a satanic cult, located in London, who were posing as druids in order to shift the blame for their evil deeds. Both contained contact information and laid claim to reward.

Upon reading the third, I said to Holmes, "You may want to have a look at this."

Taking the paper from me, he read it over several times. I can still recall each word:

"A small sacrifice at the great wall will free us all."

After Holmes had finished, he compared it to the other notes of a similar vein.

"What does it mean?"

"I should think the meaning is obvious," he replied.

"Not to me," I exclaimed.

"Think, Watson. How many 'great walls' do you know?"

"You don't mean Hadrian's Wall?"

"I do. Again, a clever diversion. As you know, Hadrian's Wall was erected in the second century to separate the Romans from the barbarians living in the north. It stretches some 73 miles from Wallsend on the River Tyne in the east to Bowness-on-Solway in the west."

"But why send us there?"

"Because it is impossible to secure. The senders are hoping that we will dispatch officers to all these different locales, thus thinning our ranks considerably, in hopes of preventing a crime."

"But what if you are wrong? What if these are legitimate warnings?"

"Sent by whom? A disenchanted druid who has no interest in the reward? No, my friend. You will notice by the way that none of communiques mentions Merlin's Mound, and that is by design, I believe. They want us panicked and running hither and yon, while they proceed about their grisly business in another locale altogether. As I have said, Watson, these are some devious minds we are dealing with here."

I found my friend's logic irrefutable, so I gave up the argument. After all, the reward was sizable and not one of the three letters had lodged a claim of any sort, a stark contrast to all of the others.

After he had read the letters over again, Holmes looked at me and said, "That seals it."

"Seals what?"

156

"I am going to visit Marlborough tomorrow. I want to familiarize myself with the terrain. I think that may allow me to make some minor modifications to Lestrade's plan and perhaps bring it more in line with my own."

"Are you planning on going alone?"

"Not if you would care to accompany me. You know how I depend upon you to see the forest while I am examining the trees."

"Was that intentional?"

"I am afraid it was. Somehow, I just couldn't resist the obvious pun."

At that point I must admit to breathing a sigh of relief. I have often remarked upon my friend's stoical nature, just as I have detailed his flair for the dramatic. Although he keeps it well-hidden, Holmes also has a lighter side that often manifests itself in wordplay. However, I have never heard such light banter pass his lips when things were looking particularly grim. That he could reveal that side of himself now gave me a feeling that no matter how dismal things might appear, Holmes would find a way to right the wrong.

"I will find someone to cover for me. What time are we leaving?"

The next morning we boarded the train for Swindon. We had made the journey once before, under rather different circumstances. Now it was just Holmes and myself, and I could see by the glint in his eye that my friend was all business. After arriving in Swindon, we hired a carriage to take us to Marlborough.

"Are you going to the college?" asked our driver.

"My colleague has some business there," said Holmes. "While he is engaged there, I thought I might wander about the village and take in the various sights."

"There's not a great deal to see in the village proper," said the driver, "except Merlin's Mound. I expect you've heard of that?"

"Fanciful nonsense," snorted Holmes.

"Aye, it is, but don't tell the tourists that come looking for it. If you've a mind, you can take in Stonehenge or perhaps Avebury. They are not too far from Marlborough."

"No," said Holmes. "I think I shall just wander the streets and enjoy the charm of your rustic village. It must be quite something with Christmas fast approaching."

"If you want Christmas celebrations, I suggest you look elsewhere. There are a few parties and such at the college, but by and large, once the students leave, it's pretty desolate until they return."

Holmes looked at me knowingly. "Really, I appear to have been misinformed," he said.

"Either that or someone is having a good laugh at your expense."

"You do have an inn where we can get rooms?" asked Holmes.

"Of course," replied the driver. "We may be rural, but we are not savages. For hearty fare and a comfortable mattress, I'd suggest the Green Dragon Inn on High Street. It's not too far from the college, and the beer is the best in town."

"Done," said Holmes.

After we had settled at the inn, Holmes and I enjoyed a light lunch before setting out to reconnoiter the grounds of the college. As we walked along High Street in the crisp air, I could only hope that we would be treated to the same kind of weather on the solstice.

We passed the various shops, a number of which had been decorated for the holidays and crossed Bath Road right onto the college grounds. The mound, impossible to miss, is located right in the center of the grounds. Holmes informed me that like Silbury Hill, it was a manmade structure, possibly the second largest in England. He also said that it had been the site for a Norman castle built by William the Conqueror in the 11th century.

There are paths around the base of the mound that eventually lead to the top. There is also a path that leads directly to the summit, although you can leave the path at any of the three levels before you arrive at the top. Approximately 60 feet high, the mound features a variety of trees growing at different spots on the various levels. Although there were a number of scrawny looking evergreens, many of the others trees had long since shed their leaves.

First, we traversed the entire hill, walking both around it to the top and then straight from the top to the bottom and then back up again. Holmes then continued to inspect the terrain for another hour or so, examining the various trees and the few bushes. He seemed to be looking for something although I must confess that I had no idea what he found so interesting.

When he had finished, Holmes looked at me and said, "It will happen here; of that I am certain."

"I do hope you are right."

"Now that I have enough facts to form a reasonable hypothesis," replied Holmes, "I know I am right."

"Then why have we been doing all this walking. You often form your theories from the comfort of your chair."

"It was imperative that I see this place, Watson. I had to put myself into the mind of the criminal. Now that I have an idea of what he may encounter on that night, I believe that I can predict how he will act and react."

"Yes, that's all well and good, I suppose, but aren't there other variables that need to be taken into account?"

"Such as?"

"How about the weather? You are here on a fine, crisp day. He will be coming here at night. He will not know the ground unless he has studied it."

"You outdo yourself, Watson. If he hasn't been here already, he will be here at least once before the solstice. This is a killer who leaves nothing to chance."

"Yes, but suppose it is pouring rain? Or we should receive an early snow?"

"I do not think mere inclemency will deter this killer from keeping his date with destiny," said Holmes. "I know for certain that it will not preclude me from mine."

Chapter 21

We enjoyed a fine dinner at the Green Dragon, and the beer was, as the driver had promised, truly excellent. The next morning, we returned to Merlin's Mound where Holmes made a second examination of the trees and bushes. He even timed himself walking to the top on the direct path.

"Once he is on the grounds, he will be alone, except for his victim," said Holmes. "Walking leisurely, I can get from the top to the bottom in about 20 seconds. Once he reaches the top, he is also out of sight, and he will be able to hear anyone approaching.

"Since he can run down any side of the hill at the first sign of danger, this is the perfect spot to commit his crime. It is isolated, and as a soldier, you can appreciate the advantage of holding the high ground."

I thought about everything Holmes said as we made our way back along High Street to collect our bags at the inn. Once again, he had summed everything up quite neatly.

"You know, Holmes," I began, "I quite understand everything that you have said, but haven't you even the slightest reservation, perhaps some niggling doubt that you may be wrong?"

I waited for an answer in vain, and then I realized that Holmes was no longer beside me. Turning back, I saw him examining the items in the window of a dry goods shop. As I started to return to him, he turned to me and we met in the middle.

"I have to thank you, Watson. Your concerns about the weather have given me an idea that may help in our efforts to bring this case to a close."

"What did I say?"

Ignoring me, Holmes said, "Two of Lestrade's men are already here, and the others will be arriving shortly. I think it imperative that we meet beforehand. Before we leave, I must send a cable to Lestrade."

When we returned to the hotel, Holmes asked me to retrieve our bags while he settled the bill. Upon arriving back in the lobby, I found him in conversation with the manager.

"Yes, we will be returning on the 22nd. I should like to reserve the same rooms if possible as well as one other."

He replied, "I don't think that will be a problem. Things get very quiet here around Christmas. After a quick look at his register, he said, "I look forward to seeing you again on the 22nd, Mr. Landon."

While we stood on the curb waiting for the carriage to take us to the station, I asked, "Did you send your cable to Lestrade?"

"Not yet," he replied. "I shall send it from Swindon. The fewer people in Marlborough who know our business, the better."

As soon as we arrived at the station in Swindon, Holmes located the telegraph office and sent his wire to Lestrade. Once we were settled in our compartment, I asked, "What was so important that you had to contact Lestrade?"

"As we walked along High Street, I kept thinking about the weather. We are asking men to spend all night out in the cold, with no shelter and no warmth. As we passed that dry goods store, I saw a variety of blankets…"

Before he could finish his sentence, I said, "Camouflage!"

"Watson, you outdo yourself. Please write this down for me. I want each of Lestrade's men to have two blankets – one of forest green and the other dark brown. They can conceal themselves using the one that better blends into their surroundings, and employ the other as they see fit to try to stay warm. I also want each man to have a dark lantern as well as a Webley."

I looked at him and said, "I shall have my service revolver, as you know, but do you really think it wise to have so many people in one place carrying pistols? Also, do you think Lestrade will be able to get permission to arm his men?"

"You cannot be serious," he replied. "We are dealing with a man who has killed thrice already, and we are hoping to prevent him from carrying out a fourth murder. This is a man with few, if any, qualms about taking innocent lives. Hopefully, the revolvers will never be employed, but I should feel terribly remiss if we did not make every attempt to provide these men with the opportunity to protect themselves."

Once again, I could see no weaknesses in Holmes' logic.

The next few days found Holmes in constant motion, and were it any other man, I might have worried about a lack of rest and proper nutrition taking its toll.

Finally on Thursday, December 21st, things slowed for Holmes. He ate a leisurely breakfast and spent the rest of the morning reading the papers, including those he had missed during his flurry of activity.

"It appears that the criminal element is conspiring with us to catch this killer," he remarked. "Three days, and not a single serious crime."

"Perhaps people are just on their best behavior with Christmas approaching."

"In all my years, I have never seen crime recognize a holiday of any sort," he added. "In fact, festive occasions seem to me, at any rate, to be the breeding grounds for any number of felonious enterprises."

I remember thinking to myself, "Sherlock Holmes can be called a great many things, but I don't think anyone would ever accuse him of being sentimental."

At about three in the afternoon, there was a rap on the door. "Come in, Lestrade," said Holmes.

After Lestrade had been seated, Holmes looked at him and said, "Is everything in place?"

"Aye, Mr. Holmes. Each of my men has purchased the blankets and a dark lantern. I have obtained permission from my superiors to equip them with guns for that one night. I also instructed each man to wear gloves; warm, dark clothing; and a hat.

"I have to thank you for your suggestion. I spoke to Sir Edward Bradford."

"And what did the Commissioner have to say?"

"He agreed that the Webleys might come in handy on this particular case, and in addition to the revolvers, each man also has a cosh – just in case. I have also asked them to purchase additional blankets and lanterns for us."

"Well done, Lestrade. And where and when are we meeting them?"

"I thought we should meet them early, so I told them to be at the Goddard Arms in Swindon at 8 a.m."

"Well that leaves us a choice," said Holmes. "We can either get up very early tomorrow or travel down there this evening."

"I was planning on going tonight," said Lestrade. "I have reserved one room, but I should be able to secure two more."

Looking at me, Holmes raised an eyebrow and said only, "Watson?"

"Well there is no time like the present," I suppose. "Just give me a few minutes to pack a bag."

"Don't dilly-dally," said Holmes. While I was in my room I could hear Holmes and Lestrade talking though I must confess that I have no idea what was said.

And so it was that Holmes, Lestrade and I once more shared a carriage as we rode from London to Swindon. While our first excursion had a definite air of excitement, based largely on the Inspector's intuition, this trip seemed far more businesslike, if such a term can be used for this endeavor. There was little chitchat, and I can still recall the look on Holmes' face as he sat there in silence.

As he had on so many other cases, he was running the endgame over and over in his mind, hoping to take into account every possible scenario – a task that given so many variables might have left a lesser man seeking help from any and all quarters. Holmes, however, sat there placidly for close to two hours.

When we finally pulled into the station at Swindon, I found it difficult to read my friend. If pressed to guess, I should say that he was satisfied with how things had progressed thus far.

After a short carriage ride from the station to the Goddard Arms, we enjoyed a dinner of roast beef with fresh vegetables and a delightful Bordeaux. Knowing that we had a long day and an even longer night in front of us on the morrow, we turned in early.

I was awakened the next morning by Holmes knocking on my door. "Come, Watson. We have much to do and little time in which to do it. I'll meet you in the dining room."

When I descended the stairs, I found Holmes and Lestrade in earnest conversation over coffee. Lestrade had ordered poached eggs and a rasher of bacon. Holmes was picking at a roll.

"The sun sets at exactly 4:33," Holmes was saying. "I think everyone should be in place no later than seven o'clock."

"That's going to be a long night in the cold," said Lestrade.

"What other choice do we have? We have no idea when he will strike, and this is our best chance to catch him before the act."

"I am not disagreeing with you, Mr. Holmes. I'm just making an observation," said Lestrade.

"Well, let's see if any of your men have any better suggestions," said Holmes.

After we finished our breakfast, we retired to a room in the back of the house that I am guessing was used for socials and the like. Holmes spread out a large map across the table, securing the edges with books and a set of candlesticks.

He had just finished when there was a knock on the door and two strapping fellows entered. "Ah, Driscoll and Hutchinson," said Lestrade. "You are prompt."

"The others will be along momentarily," said the one who had been identified as Driscoll. "We saw them on the road behind us."

Lestrade then introduced the two officers to Holmes and myself. A few minutes later, there was a knock on the door, and three more men entered. They were all tall and exuded an air of confidence and subtle menace. I do not think I should have liked to take their measure, and was quite glad that they were on our side.

After we had been introduced to Sergeants Porter, Tierney and Driver, Lestrade began by saying, "Once again, I want to thank you for volunteering for this assignment. We face a long, difficult night, but I am hopeful that we can bring this case to a close.

"As you know, Mr. Sherlock Holmes has proved invaluable to the Yard on any number of occasions in the past, and he and Dr. Watson will be will be with us tonight.

"Together, Holmes and I have devised a plan that at its worst will result in the capture of this so-called druidic killer, and with some luck, we may also be able to save a life tonight. I'll let Mr. Holmes explain the finer points of the plan to you. Just know that you have earned the gratitude of those who are aware of the sacrifices you have made and will make tonight."

Holmes looked at the men and said, "Gentlemen, we are facing a most dangerous adversary tonight. We know that he has killed at least three times previously, perhaps more.

"I fully expect him to take his victim to the top of Merlin's Mound. You are all familiar with the area?" There were nods all around the table. "Excellent, here is what I propose we do. Dr. Watson and I will be on the topmost level of the mound. We will conceal ourselves at opposite ends. Inspector Lestrade and Sergeant Tierney will conceal themselves on the other two sides. If all goes according to plan, he will be totally surrounded.

"Now, you others will station yourselves at these spots," said Holmes, indicating four different locations, one on each side, at the base of the mound. Should the fiend escape our trap on the top level, it will be up to one of you to make certain that he does not get away entirely.

"You have all secured the blankets and dark lanterns?" Again, there were nods of assent. "I believe Inspector Lestrade has something else for you men."

"Actually, I have two things for you," said Lestrade as he placed a satchel on the table. Opening the bag, he began to pull out the Webleys, handing one with an extra box of cartridges to each man. When he had finished, he said, "Permission to carry these comes directly from Commission Bradford, and that should be an indication of how badly he wants this man captured. We will be in the dark, so think of these as the last resort. Remember, your comrades might be moving, so be absolutely certain that you have the killer in your sights should you feel the need to fire."

There were looks of gratitude, mixed with a hint of disbelief as Lestrade parceled out the weapons. When he had finished, Sergeant Driver said, "Speaking for all of us, thank you sir."

"And you all have your coshes?" asked Lestrade.

"We do," said Driver. "You said there were two things Inspector."

"I did, indeed," said Lestrade. Reaching into the satchel once again, he pulled out five Masonic flasks. "It's going to be a long night, so before you take your positions, fill these with hot tea or coffee. Hopefully, tomorrow we can celebrate with something a bit stronger."

"You all have your whistles?" asked Holmes, "and you know the signals?"

"We do, sir," said Tierney, who together with Driver appeared to be the two senior officers.

After Holmes and Lestrade had fielded a few more questions, they went over the plan one more time. When they had finished, Holmes looked at them and said, "Be careful, gentlemen. We are dealing with an adversary unlike any other you may have encountered.

"It's going to be a long, cold night, so get some rest and then everybody should be in position no later than seven o'clock. Good luck, men."

As they left, I was a whirl of emotions. I felt the excitement of the chase, but it was tempered by the fact that these brave men had volunteered to try to catch a killer. I didn't know if they had families or not, but I was grateful that such men stood between us and this and sundry other unspeakable evils.

Suddenly, I felt Holmes staring at me. Without saying a word, he simply glanced at the men then back and me and gave an almost imperceptible nod. At that point, I knew that the day was going to drag on inexorably. When we left the inn to depart for Marlborough, the sky was gray and overcast. Throughout the carriage ride, I could feel the burden of time on my shoulders. I saw much the same look on Lestrade's face, but Holmes was a veritable picture of equanimity. I then determined to enjoy the respite because I knew that an uncertain future awaited us at the top of Merlin's Mound.

Chapter 22

"And you must promise me that you will be careful? We are so close!" she implored.

"I promise you that I will come to no harm, acushla," he replied.

"How can you be so sure?"

"Because we have been through this before. I have taken every precaution. There are ample diversions out there. The police will be hunting for me from one end of the country to the other, but I do not think, they will be where I am."

"And have you the branches? And the symbol and the message?"

Pointing to a pack he had slung over his horse's back, he said, "I cut them this morning. Everything I need is right there. Once this is done, we are in the clear, and no one will ever suspect us. I promise you that."

"I do hope that you are right," she said. "I don't know what I would do if anything were to happen to you."

"Well you needn't worry yourself. Now I must go. I have a great many miles to cover if I am to finish this business."

"I don't want to know anything else," she exclaimed. "I just want to know that when the sun rises tomorrow, you will be here with me – safe and sound."

"I give you my word," he said, and before she could say anything else, he wheeled his horse around and headed for his destination.

As he rode, he considered everything that had happened in the past nine months, and then he cast his mind back even further, remembering the first time he had seen her so many years before and how totally smitten he had been.

It was a match that never would have happened. He, the son of a poor dairy farmer, and she, the daughter of the local gentry. Despite everything, their love had triumphed, and he would do anything, even the darkest deeds, for her.

Although the years of separation had been difficult, the travails he had undergone while abroad had changed him, and he had returned from Africa and his service in Dahomey a vastly different man. Life meant more to him than it ever had, and if taking another to advance his own were required, then so be it. He had long since given up thoughts of an afterlife. The only things that really mattered were the here and the now. They were reality, not some vague promise of eternity that might never come to fruition.

However, the pain that he had endured paled in comparison to the joy he felt when he thought of her. Time had done nothing to cool their ardor, and when he had chanced to see her on Marylebone Road in London that spring day three years ago, it was as if an hour had passed instead of more than two decades.

And then he turned his thoughts to their future together. He reasoned that the bonds that had joined them – as unseemly as they now might be – had been forged of iron. Certainly, they were far firmer than any words he might have muttered standing in a church somewhere. They had both been tested and they had emerged victorious – and together.

No, the future looked bright and promising and all that stood between him and the woman he loved were the deeds of one more night.

Steeling himself for the task ahead, he spurred his horse on. "The sooner this is behind us, the better."

Chapter 23

Our carriage deposited us in front of the Green Dragon, and the manager seemed quite pleased to see us again, especially since there were now three of us. The hotel seemed remarkably quiet, and then I remembered it was the Friday before the Christmas holiday.

After Holmes suggested that we meet at six for dinner, we all retired to our rooms to get some rest. I cannot speak for Holmes or Lestrade, but for a long time sleep eluded me as surely as this killer had sidestepped all of our efforts to capture him. So I lay there, turning over all the events of the past nine months, reviewing each murder in detail and wondering what Holmes had seen that I had not. When I finally did nod off, my dreams were filled with gruesome images and druidic symbols.

When I awoke, I glanced at my watch and saw that it was just ten minutes before six. I quickly washed my face and went downstairs to meet Holmes and Lestrade.

Dinner was a solemn affair. We sat off in a corner of the dining room so that Holmes and Lestrade could review their plans one final time. Anytime someone would enter the dining room, he attracted the attention of my friend, who would appraise the individual and then dismiss him.

The meal might have been a feast, but my mind was racing to the night ahead. As a result, I tasted little although, oddly enough, Holmes seemed to enjoy his food as did Lestrade.

As we sat over coffee and cigars, the inspector said, "Best savor that Mr. Holmes. It might be a while before we can enjoy another."

"True enough," he replied. Pulling his watch from his pocket, he said, "It is a quarter before the hour. I suggest that we make our way to the mound." Each of us then returned to our rooms where we retrieved the blankets the officers had given us earlier in the day. I checked to make certain that I had an extra candle and matches for my dark lantern. I put everything in a small satchel and then I took the flask downstairs and asked if I might have it filled with hot tea.

"What might you gentlemen be up to this evening?" inquired the manager. I could see that Holmes and Lestrade were carrying similar bags and assumed that they had made identical requests.

"Tonight is the winter solstice," replied Holmes. "And we are going over to Avebury to record the constellations and take photographs of the sunrise with a revolutionary new camera that my friend here is developing," said Holmes, indicating Lestrade.

"Well, I wish you the best of luck," he replied. "Hopefully, the rain will hold off, and there will be a sunrise to photograph; otherwise, you will have spent a night in the cold for nothing."

"Such are the vagaries of nature," replied Holmes. "We are at the mercy of forces beyond our control."

A few minutes later, we found ourselves walking along High Street toward the grounds of Marlborough College. What had been such a pleasant excursion just a few days earlier, now seemed fraught with peril.

When we entered the grounds, we were in total darkness. The clouds hid the stars, and there were no lanterns on the pathways. Holmes took the lead, walking slowly, followed by Lestrade, and I brought up the rear.

We headed straight to the path that led to the top. How different things seemed under the cover of darkness. I imagined blackguards and cutthroats lurking behind every bush and tree. I must confess that it took me a minute to rein in my imagination. "Thoughts like that will do you no good on a night like this," I told myself.

Although Merlin's Mound is but sixty feet high, give or take, that climb seemed far longer than it was. Each step was taken with care. When we finally reached the summit, I thought I saw something move in the shadows to our left and then Sergeant Tierney materialized out of the darkness. "All the men are in place below," he said.

"Excellent," said Holmes. "Let us make a square – one on each side of the summit at the outermost edges where there are trees and bushes for concealment. Lestrade, you take the far end. Watson and Sergeant Tierney will face each other from opposite sides, and I will remain here, closest to the path.

"I do not know how long we must wait, but I cannot impress upon you strongly enough the need for absolute silence."

We then moved to our places. I found myself on Holmes' right side. After some little searching, I discovered a small bush that still had a surprising number of leaves on it and wrapped myself in my blankets, with the green one on the outside.

With nothing to do but wait, I started to think back over my long association with Holmes. We had faced thieves, blackmailers and more than our share of murderers, but I could recall no one who had ever killed in this manner before save the Ripper. I knew that Holmes had long since jettisoned the secret cult of druids theory, and I began to wonder what had led him to his conclusions.

After a few hours, the cold began to creep into my bones. Although I listened intently, I could not hear a sound. I stretched as silently as I could and shook my limbs, trying to keep warm. I was fully aware that I might have to leap into action at any time.

As I waited, I recalled other vigils with Holmes. I was just about to take a sip of tea when I thought I heard a voice. I remained absolutely still until I heard it a second time. Although I couldn't see anything, I could now make out the words: "Careful there laddie, you've had a wee bit too much to drink. Watch your step there now."

The voices were coming from the direction of the path we had used to ascend to the top. "Almost there, my boy. Just a few more steps."

I strained my eyes to see in the darkness, and on the other side of the plateau, I saw a single lantern come into view. The light was not bright, but in that absolute darkness it seemed a brilliant beacon. I could discern two figures, one taller than the other, and the taller one seemed to be almost dragging the other one along with him.

They moved to the center of the top level, where the taller figure placed the other one on the ground. He then proceeded to unpack a bag he had been carrying, although for the life of me I could not see what it contained.

After he had placed the various items on the ground near the other figure, I saw him lift something and then he spoke, "*Nos morituri te salutamus.*" Since he was facing in my direction, I could see what he was doing thanks to the light of his lantern. I saw him take a long drink from a silver flask, and then he pulled a knife from his belt.

At the point I heard Holmes declare, "I don't think anyone need die here tonight."

The man then whirled and threw his lantern at Holmes. When it hit the ground, it went out and pandemonium reigned.

I heard Lestrade yell, "Don't you move!"

In the darkness, I heard the sound of footsteps running; I can only assume they were the killer's as he tried to make his escape. Then Sergeant Tierney yelled, "He's heading down the path, I think." With that he began to blow his police whistle.

Holmes then yelled, "Watson, see to the victim." I managed to light my dark lantern and by its glow, I soon found a young man of about 20, unconscious in the middle of the clearing. I could feel a pulse, and although I could find no puncture wound on the neck, I thought that he might have been drugged.

I lifted him to a sitting position, and tried to get a bit of tea into him to no avail. With all my strength, I managed to get him standing and started to walk him about, hoping the increased blood flow might help to dispel the effects of whatever he had been given. All the while, I could hear shouts in the darkness.

"He's headed your way, Driver."

"No one has come past me."

"Over there," yelled Sergeant Driscoll.

"We can't let him escape," I heard Lestrade yell.

The shouts continued back and forth and then suddenly, I felt a hand on my shoulder. When I turned around, Holmes was standing there holding his dark lantern.

"How is he?"

"I think he's been drugged, but once that wears off, he should be fine. Why aren't you helping with the chase?"

"Our quarry is long gone, I fear," replied my friend. "This is what I wanted," he said, leaning down and picking up the bag left behind by the would-be killer.

"Is that important?"

"Unless, I miss my guess, the contents of this bag should tell us with absolute certainty the identity of the killer. Moreover, it will tell us where to find him and it may also reveal the identity of his accomplice."

Chapter 24

While the officers and Lestrade continued to scour the countryside, Holmes and I headed back to the Green Dragon with our new companion. Between the two of us, we virtually carried him back to the inn, and the owner was none too happy to be awakened from his bed by Holmes pounding on the door.

"I thought you gentlemen were going to Avebury," he said. "And what has happened to poor Samuel here?"

Holmes quickly filled him in, judiciously omitting some key facts and improvising on other aspects. We soon retired to the dining room, where after I had administered some smelling salts Samuel began to regain consciousness. At that point, a bit of brandy brought him fully around.

He told us that he had met a stranger, an Irishman, who had introduced himself as Liam O'Day, in a pub. They got to talking about horses and the approaching holiday, and the next thing Samuel remembered was waking up in the dining room with us.

"Can you describe this Mr. O'Day for us?" asked Holmes.

"He was quite tall with dark black hair and blue eyes. He had a scar on his left cheek, and he said he was on his way to London to visit a sister."

Holmes asked a number of other questions, and he concluded with, "Did you happen to notice is he was left- or right-handed?"

"He was left-handed," replied Samuel. At that moment, Lestrade and the other officers came into the inn. "He got clean away, Mister Holmes. How he did it I'll never know, for we had the mound surrounded."

"Don't worry Lestrade," he won't get too far.

"How can you say that?"

"Because he left this behind," said Holmes, placing the case on the table.

"What good will that do us?"

"Unless I am very much mistaken, it will tell us where to find him. Sergeant Driscoll would you escort Samuel home?"

Looking at the youngster, Holmes said, "You are one lucky lad, but from now on, you would do well to be wary of strangers bearing drinks."

After they had left, Lestrade looked at the satchel and said, "Will that really lead us to the killer?"

Opening it, Holmes pulled out a piece of piece of paper. At the top was another druidic symbol.

"Here's the first bit of evidence that Mr. O'Day was our druid of death."

"What does that mean?" asked Lestrade.

"It's a rough version of a Celtic cross," replied Holmes. "It can mean many things depending upon how you interpret it. Some see it as a navigational tool, others see it as the meeting of energies; still others see it as a symbol of transition. I think the latter interpretation is the one we were intended to ascribe to it. The victim was intended to move from life to death on this night just as the year moves from death to life, with the days starting to grow longer immediately."

"But what does it all mean?" Lestrade almost roared.

"Quite frankly, it means nothing," replied Holmes, "but I will get to that in a moment." Looking at the paper, Holmes said, "Here is the second indication. You can see the ogham writing here as well."

"And does that mean nothing, as well?" asked Lestrade.

"Don't hold me to this translation," said Holmes, "but I think it may be translated as 'the end'."

"The end? The end of what?"

"The end of this charade," replied Holmes.

"Once again, Mr. Holmes. I am at your mercy," said Lestrade.

"Wait, there are a few more things to consider," said Holmes.

First, he pulled a small box out of the bag and when he opened the case, we saw a syringe and two small vials of what I believed was some sort of opiate. "I'm sure he brought this along, just in case Samuel started to come around."

"Is there anything else?"

"Of course," said Holmes, who then pulled several small evergreen branches from the bag. "This is what I really wanted you to see, Lestrade."

"Branches? There have been branches at every murder."

"But none quite like these."

"And what makes those so special?"

"The trees from which they were cut."

"Oh, Mr. Holmes. I am really starting to worry about you. We have here a few branches from a Christmas tree, and you are telling me that these will lead us to our murderer."

"These are not just Christmas tree branches, as you put it Lestrade. These branches have been cut from a Douglas fir. As you know, I dabble a bit in botany and could bore you with the story about the Scottish botanist David Douglas and his rival, Archibald Menzies, but I digress. The important thing to remember is that the Douglas fir is distinctive in having cones that exhibit a long tridentine bract that protrudes prominently above each scale, just as these cuttings do, Consider, it almost resembles the back half of a mouse, with two feet and a tail."

"Oh, Mr. Holmes, after a disappointing night such as we have just had, I must warn you that my patience is just about gone. For the love of God, please make yourself plain about the importance of these branches.

As Holmes spoke, it soon became apparent to everyone in the room that he knew exactly where the branches had come from and how they related to the attempted murder.

"So all we have to do then is go pick them up," said Lestrade.

"If only it were that simple," replied Holmes.

"Well, what's to stop us?"

Holmes then explained how our efforts might be met with skepticism for certain – if not outright resistance.

"So then what's to be done?" asked Lestrade.

Holmes then outlined exactly how he wanted to proceed. When he had finished, he looked at Lestrade and asked, "Do you still believe in me?"

"In for a penny, in for a pound," replied Lestrade. And with that we began ironing out the rough spots in Holmes' plan and formulating a way that we might apprehend the guilty parties without placing anyone else in jeopardy or besmirching the good name of Scotland Yard.

Chapter 25

For the next two weeks, we did absolutely nothing. I could see that Lestrade was chafing under the yoke of inactivity. With each visit to our lodgings, he grew increasingly anxious to be about the business of the law, as he put it.

"Lestrade, they suffered a bad scare on the winter solstice. You came quite close to apprehending the killer," said Holmes, trying to console him.

"Exactly, my point. What's makes you think they aren't in the wind and heading for some remote section of Europe or that they haven't already set sail for America or Australia?"

"They killed for a very specific reason," said Holmes.

"A reason you are not willing to share with me," replied Lestrade rather tartly.

"I am keeping you in the dark for your own safety," replied Holmes. "I need the killers to feel safe and secure. They must think that they have gotten away clean. There can be no word of this or they *will* be on that ship you mentioned. And if there were a slip-up, it very well might mean your job. You've trusted me thus far; just a bit longer, old friend."

I could see that Lestrade was unhappy but he nodded his head and acquiesced to my friend.

Three days later, I awoke to find a note from Holmes on the breakfast table.

Watson,

I have decided to spend a day in the countryside communing with nature. I will see you this evening. Please ask Mrs. Hudson to hold dinner for me.

Yours,

S.H.

What a curious note, I thought to myself. As I have often remarked, Holmes eschewed exercise for its own sake and the thought of the finest brain in London "communing with nature" as he put it was, I must admit, rather a difficult concept for me to grasp.

Still, I had known Holmes to undertake even stranger endeavors in the name of his chosen profession. I also knew that if he were successful in whatever quest he might be on that he would be unable to refrain from telling me about it.

I spent the morning recording my notes on this adventure and then writing up my notes from one of Holmes' lesser exploits, "The Curious Cask of Curzon Street." After that, I treated myself to lunch at the Criterion where I handed the "Curzon" pages over to my literary agent for his consideration. After leaving my old haunt, I strolled back to Baker Street where I spent the rest of the afternoon re-reading and revising my notes on this case. It was just after five when I heard Holmes on the stairs and he burst into our rooms with a huge smile on his face. I knew that something important had broken his way, and was debating whether to ask him what had transpired or let him tell me in his own manner.

I decided once again to indulge my friend's flair for the dramatic and let him tell me what had occurred when he was ready. He threw himself into his chair, fished out his cigarettes and asked me for a match.

After lighting his cigarette, he looked at me and asked with a practiced nonchalance, "Is the fare at the Criterion still top-shelf? I have heard a few people express misgivings about it lately."

"How on earth could you know where I have been?"

"You have just handed me a new pack of Swan Vestas and while there are several establishments in London that provide them to patrons, the only one I know that you frequent is the Criterion."

"Blast it, do you never tire of being right? Yes, I did dine there, and yes, the food is as good as it ever was in my opinion."

"And your companion, does he share your enthusiasm for the fare?"

"How could you possibly know that I dined with a friend?"

"The pile of notes that was on your desk early this morning is there no longer, having been replaced by a new, smaller stack of notes that you were working on when I arrived. The only one who has any interest in your writings before they are published is your agent. Therefore I can only conclude that you dined with him and submitted another of my cases for possible publication."

"You never miss a trick, do you?"

"Oh, I have missed a great many tricks on this case, but I am trying to atone for my shortcomings as best I can."

"You are too hard on yourself. Scotland Yard has …"

He interrupted me by asking, "Surely, you are not comparing my efforts to those of Lestrade and his crew?"

"Not at all; it's just that…"

"No explanation is necessary, Watson. This has been far from my finest hour, but we may still salvage something of our reputations."

"Well, since you know where I have been all day, would you care to tell me what it was you were doing?"

"I have been collecting evidence," he said, opening the bag he carried and placing an evergreen branch on the table. "Does this look familiar?"

"Indeed, it looks just like the branches we confiscated on the winter solstice."

"Exactly. In fact, this particular branch probably came from the exact same tree that provided our killer with two of his cuttings."

"In all of England, how could you possibly know which tree to examine?"

"One of the things I neglected to mention about the Douglas fir is that it is a relatively new tree to England."

"Extraordinary!"

"And that is where my knowledge of botany comes into play. Any botanist worth his salt will tell you that our fair isle is home to only three native species of conifer trees – the Scots pine, the yew and the common juniper. As a result, the Douglas fir, though it is catching on, is still relatively rare here. Native to North America, the Douglas fir was introduced into England in 1827 by that Scottish botanist David Douglas.

"If you know what to look for, it is relatively easy to spot. We had seen a magnificent stand of such trees during ..."

"Our visit to the estate of Lady Deveron."

"Indeed. In fact, I believe that I remarked upon them at the time. Earlier today, I took a rather circuitous route onto the estate and was able to inspect the trees at my leisure. I discovered that several low-hanging branches had been cut from different trees. Having brought along a small saw, I cut this one for comparison."

"You mean Lady Deveron has been involved with the killings?"

"That remains to be determined, although all inclinations would seem to indicate so."

"She may have been coerced or she may have been duped," I said.

"Always the knight in shining armor. I will grant you that possibility, but of this I am certain – someone in her employ has played an active role in the slayings."

"To what end?"

"There we must venture into the realm of speculation. As you know that is something I am loath to do. But I have been gathering evidence and collecting facts, and I think it is about time that we paid another call on Her Ladyship."

"Now, let me send a wire to Lestrade, and then we can enjoy our dinner. Nothing like a long walk in the fresh country air to build up an appetite."

And so it was that early the next morning, Holmes, Lestrade and I again boarded a train at Paddington. The trip took about four hours, and Lestrade peppered Holmes with questions for much of the journey. By the time we had arrived, I knew that Lestrade and Holmes were of one mind, and both agreed that there were several loose ends that needed to be tied up.

Lestrade had wired ahead to Her Ladyship, telling her that there had been some developments in the case of her stepson's death.

When we arrived at the estate, the gatekeeper was waiting for us and informed us that Her Ladyship was indeed expecting us.

As we drove toward the house, I was once again overwhelmed by the vastness of the grounds. "It is a veritable arboretum," I remarked.

"Yes," replied Holmes, "and I shouldn't wonder that the various trees served as a source of inspiration."

As we neared the house, I found myself fixated on the stand of Douglas fir that had captured my attention on our first visit. I nudged Holmes, who followed my gaze to the trees, and then nodded imperceptibly in my direction.

The same servant greeted us at the front door, and escorted us to the same room where we had met with Her Ladyship on our previous visit.

We had been sitting for a few minutes when she entered. She was again dressed all in black, and I was struck once more with how well she appeared to be holding up.

We rose and Holmes introduced Lestrade. Her Ladyship began by stating, "I understand that you have news for me."

"Indeed," said Holmes, looking at Lestrade. "We came very close to catching this druid killer on the night of the winter solstice. Unfortunately, he managed to escape despite our best efforts to apprehend him."

"Where was that?"

"The assault took place on a young man from Marlborough on the top of a historic site the locals call Merlin's Mound. As you might expect, the location of the attack and all the particulars are in accordance with the earlier killings."

"Have you any idea where the killer is now?"

Holmes replied, "We have tracked the suspect to the Continent, but in Calais he was able to elude his pursuers. For the moment we are endeavoring to pick up the scent again, and you may rest assured that we will not rest until he is brought to justice."

"Does this person have a name?" asked Her Ladyship.

"He is known as Lawrence Mayweather. He is an itinerant Scotsman who has been working hard to revive the flames of the old pagan religion. Do you know if your stepson ever spoke of such a man?"

"Not that I can recall," said Her Ladyship, "but Trent was always a very private boy."

"Ah, that explains it perhaps," said Holmes.

"Was my offer of a reward any help?"

"It provided us with a number of false trails and one or two interesting letters, but I regret to inform you that ultimately the offer did not factor into our efforts."

"Then I am sorry that it proved more of a distraction than an incentive," she replied.

"It was a noble effort," said Lestrade.

Although Her Ladyship asked us to stay for lunch, we declined. Holmes said he had to return to London to attend to another pressing case. After we had said our farewells, we walked down the long gallery and Holmes once again paused by the painting that had attracted his attention on our last visit. This time, he only examined it for a few seconds, and then we made our way downstairs where our cab was waiting for us.

After we had left the grounds, we started back in the direction of Bath. We hadn't gone but half a mile when Holmes bade the driver to pull over to the side of the road.

After he had done so, the driver looked at us and asked, "Now what, guv?"

"I want you to climb down and try to look as though you are working on one of the rear wheels. And if you ask no more questions, there'll be an extra pound in it for you."

The driver happily set about examining the rear wheel on the road side while Holmes, Lestrade and I climbed out and stood on the other side.

"And now we wait?" asked Lestrade.

"Unless I have missed the mark altogether, we shan't have too long a stay here," said Holmes. "The difficulty is in guessing the direction."

"Which direction?" I asked.

"Whether Her Ladyship will send her messenger to Bath or Bristol," replied Holmes.

Before he could answer, we saw a rider on a large black stallion leave the grounds of Ravenhurst and set out at a full gallop in our direction.

"Our luck holds," said Holmes. "Driver, how are you doing with that wheel?" Holmes asked as the horseman, who took no notice of us, sped by.

As soon as the rider was out of earshot, Holmes exclaimed "To Bath with all due speed!"

No sooner had we clambered aboard than the driver turned to us and asked, "Any place in particular?"

"We will start at the Saracens Head, and if you are as sharp as I think you are, there may be a bit of extra work in it for you."

When we disembarked at the Saracens Head, Holmes spoke briefly with the driver. I could not hear what was said, but I could easily discern the urgency in my friend's voice.

After he had finished, he turned to Lestrade and me and said, "I don't know about you but I am parched. I have it on good authority that this inn possesses not only a fine selection of ales but a rather impressive wine cellar as well. Shall we?"

As we sat there, I had a million questions swirling in my mind. Looking at Lestrade, I could see that he was as vexed as I was.

After we had been served, Lestrade took a long drink of ale and then said as patiently as he could, "I believe that we are entitled to an explanation, Mr. Holmes."

"Indeed, you are," said my friend. "The rider who passed was a messenger from Lady Deveron to her lover. It is her paramour who has actually committed the murders."

"Lawrence Mayweather," I exclaimed.

"Who?" asked Holmes, and then he began to chuckle.

"Isn't Mayweather the name of the man we seek? That's what you told Her Ladyship."

"And so I did, but that was to put her at ease. I made up the name Lawrence Mayweather. I believe that we are looking for a fellow by the name of Liam O'Dowd."

"The fellow who drugged Samuel in Marlborough?" asked Lestrade.

Holmes then proceeded to tell us what he had learned about O'Dowd, and the fellow's relationship to Lady Deveron. When he had finished, Lestrade asked, "So is she his accomplice?"

"That last little bit continues to elude me," said Holmes, "and I will not comment on it until I am absolutely certain. Slander is a serious offense, and I should hate to be accused of willfully besmirching the name of a member of the nobility – at least not until I am satisfied that she is guilty."

Despite vows of silence from both Lestrade and myself, Holmes remained adamant. Finally, he looked at us and said, "If Her Ladyship is innocent and I were sued, you might be called to the stand to testify against me. If I have said nothing, you can say nothing. This is a burden that I must bear alone."

I have often remarked on the nobility of Holmes' nature, but in that moment it shone as brilliantly as his intellect towered above others. I could see that he would have liked nothing more than to discuss it with us, but he understood that to do so might place us in a precarious position with the law at some point in the future. I don't think I have ever been more proud of my friend.

We had just about finished our ales when the driver who had brought us to town poked his head through the door. Upon seeing Holmes, he started to enter the room. Holmes rose and met him halfway. There was a brief but hushed conversation, and I saw my friend press some notes into the man's hand.

When Holmes returned to the table, Lestrade asked, "What was that all about?"

"I believe that Mr. O'Dowd is now renting a room above the Star Inn on The Paragon."

"Well, if he is there, I should very much like to pay him a visit," said Lestrade.

"And so you shall, my friend. I have no idea whether he knows Watson or myself, but as today was your first visit to Ravenhurst, and he was absent, we can be reasonably certain that he does not know you."

Holmes then explained the part that each of us would play and how he hoped the evening would unfold. When he had finished, he looked at us and said, "Justice has been a long time coming for Liam O'Dowd, but I believe that day has finally arrived."

Chapter 26

When I entered the Star Inn at around six that evening, as per Holmes' instructions, I had no idea what to expect. The inn dates back several centuries, and, under different circumstances, I could imagine myself spending a pleasant evening here with Holmes and Lestrade.

Upon arriving, I looked for Holmes and spotted him sitting in the corner hidden behind a newspaper. When I turned my attention to the bar, I was a bit surprised to see Lestrade manning the taps. He was wearing a colorful vest with his sleeves rolled up and his tie missing. I must admit that he looked every inch the country innkeeper.

There were a few other men in the room, but they were busy playing cards or dominoes. I made my way to the bar where Lestrade asked, "What can I get for you, stranger?" I ordered a pint of ale and then sat at the table nearest the doorway. I patted my pocket just to reassure myself that I had remembered to bring my sidearm.

There was little conversation in the room, and so, like Holmes, I pretended to read my newspaper. We had been there about an hour when a tall dark-haired man entered, and took a seat at the bar. "You're new here aren't you?" he asked Lestrade in a broad Irish accent. "Where's George?"

"He was called away on some sort of a family emergency," replied Lestrade. "Can I get you something?"

"I'd like a pint of ale and a shepherd's pie," replied the stranger.

Drawing the pint, Lestrade said, "Just let me check in the kitchen on your pie."

While he was gone, the stranger surveyed the room, and apparently there was nothing there that alarmed him, for he soon returned to his pint and a consideration of the bottles behind the bar.

Lestrade returned a minute later and said, "You're in luck. You've ordered the last one, so they just have to warm it up and it should be ready in no time. Will you be eating it here or taking it to a table?"

"I'll eat here if you don't mind."

"Not at all," replied Lestrade. "It's slow tonight, as you can see, so there is plenty of room. We have some fresh-made cabbage soup if that appeals to you while you're waiting."

"I haven't had cabbage soup in a long time," replied the stranger. "A small bowl if you please."

Lestrade disappeared into the kitchen, returning a few minutes later carrying a tray on which sat a bowl. As he started to place a napkin on the bar, one of the men left his table and stood to the stranger's left. "After you've finished, I'd like two more pints," he said.

"I'll be with you momentarily," said Lestrade.

He then bent beneath the bar, at which point, I said, "And I'll have another as well."

When the stranger turned to look at me, Holmes bolted from his seat and pinned the man's right arm to the bar even as the man on his other side held the left arm firmly against the counter. Lestrade arose from behind the bar, and before you could say "nicked," he had slapped a pair of handcuffs on the man.

"Liam O'Dowd, you are under arrest for the murders of Annie Lock, Jeremy Mason and the Honorable Trent Deveron."

196

"There must be some mistake," O'Dowd replied. "I have no idea who any of those people are?"

"Do you know Lady Deveron?" asked Lestrade.

There was a slight pause before he answered, "I have heard of her, certainly. Who hasn't? But as for knowing her ..."

"Mr. O'Dowd," said Holmes, "she sent you a message earlier today. Perhaps if we search your room, we will come across the missive."

O'Dowd appeared to ready to brazen it out. "You may search my room as well as my person. You will find no note from Her Ladyship or anyone else."

"Why don't you save us the trouble?" asked Holmes. "I will find the note eventually."

At that point, O'Dowd tried to break free from his captors and lunge at Holmes, but he was quickly restrained. "Take him to the jail," Lestrade ordered the two men, whom I soon discovered were local constables. As they led him from the bar, O'Dowd looked back over his shoulder and said, "I've done nothing, and you will find nothing."

"Lestrade, do go along with the constables and make certain that he has not concealed the note somewhere on his person. Should you discover it, please let me know at once. In the meantime, Watson and I will conduct a thorough search of his room.'"

"And you are certain there is a note?" asked Lestrade.

"He was contacted by Her Ladyship. Unless he has eaten it, which I doubt, we must find that note. I am certain that it will give us a clue as to whether Her Ladyship is involved."

After they had left, Holmes and I ascended to O'Dowd's room on the second floor. It was a fairly Spartan affair, containing only a bed, chair, desk, bureau and wastebasket. There were also a few books, a closet in which his clothes had been stored and a crucifix on the wall.

Holmes pulled the chair into the center of the room, steepled his fingers under his chin and began to concentrate.

After I had examined all the obvious places, including the wastebasket, desk and bureau drawers, various books and the backs of the pictures hanging on the wall, I turned to Holmes and said, "You know he may have thrown it down the privy."

Holmes who had not spoken the entire time I was searching, looked at me and said simply, "That won't do. Suppose you were O'Dowd," said Holmes, "and your lover had sent you a missive – on the off-chance that it might be the last communication you received from her, wouldn't you save it, treasure it?"

"So now he and Lady Deveron are lovers?"

"Of course, they are. Anyone could see that she has been involved in this from the beginning."

"I must confess, I couldn't."

"What did you just say?"

"I said, 'I must confess, I couldn't'."

Holmes looked at me and asked, "Is there by chance a small painting of any kind in that closet. Or does it contain just his clothes?"

"Let me take another look." Upon giving the closet a much closer examination, I discovered that a small still-life had been pushed to the back of a shelf where it might have remained unseen, had Holmes not inquired about it. "How on earth could you possibly know?"

Holmes smiled, "Does O'Dowd strike you as a religious man?"

"Not if he has killed three people," I replied.

"Exactly," said Holmes. "Yet he has a crucifix hanging above his bed."

"What of it?" I asked. "Perhaps the landlord put it there."

"Perhaps," said Holmes, "but given the rather subtle Freemason symbol that rests above the bar, I rather doubt he is inclined to sympathize with the papacy." As he said this, he rose and removed the icon from the wall. Bringing it closer to the light, he began to examine it. Suddenly, the figure of Christ and the top piece of wood slid up, revealing a hidden compartment.

"What on Earth!"

"This is what the Catholics refer to as a sick-call set," explained Holmes. "Normally, one might expect to find candles and a vial of holy water. People keep them on hand in case they should need a priest in a hurry. When he arrives, everything he needs to perform the last rites is at hand."

"Ingenious," I said.

"No, what's ingenious is the use to which our friend O'Dowd has put it."

Looking over Holmes shoulder, I could see that the secret recess in the cross contained two small vials as well as a tightly rolled-up scrap of paper.

"Unless I am very much mistaken, those are extra vials of the drug O'Dowd used on his victims, and this should be the note from Her Ladyship."

Unrolling the piece of paper, I saw that the note had been written in ogham. I have reproduced the message below.

"Blast," said Holmes. "I should have expected this. The ogham may prove our undoing."

"This is a college town. Surely there must be someone who can translate it for us."

"Excellent, Watson. We must try O'Dowd first and then, if he proves uncooperative, as I suspect he will, perhaps there is a faculty member who is familiar with the language."

Holmes and I then proceeded to the local jail where we were met by a beaming Lestrade. "I never doubted you, Mr. Holmes, and I cannot thank you enough."

"Don't thank me yet, Lestrade. The job is only half-done."

"What do you mean?"

"From the very start, I suspected there were at least two people involved. Yes, we have the killer, but I want his accomplice as well."

"And who might that be?"

"When the time is ripe," replied Holmes. "For the moment, I should like to question O'Dowd. Perhaps he will be more forthcoming with someone who is not attached to the official police."

"Before we go any further, do we have any new evidence?" asked Lestrade.

Holmes showed him the crucifix with the hidden compartment. "I am certain that if you test these two vials they will prove to be the same drug that we found in the bag on Merlin's Mound. We also have this note written in ogham."

"What does it say?" asked Lestrade.

"That is what I am hoping Mr. O'Dowd will tell me. Now, Lestrade, time is of the essence here."

We then went back to the cell where O'Dowd was being held. Holmes looked at him and said, "I must confess that hiding the note in the crucifix was a stroke of brilliance, but I did discover it, nonetheless. I don't suppose you would be kind enough to translate it for us?"

O'Dowd said nothing, merely glowering at Holmes from the cot on which he sat.

"We have you. We have the knife used in the killings which was in the bag you dropped on Merlin's Mound. I am certain the drugs in the crucifix will also match those in the bag. You will certainly go to the gallows for those murders. Do you really want your accomplice to enjoy the fruits of your labors – perhaps with another man?"

Despite Holmes' best efforts, he could not get O'Dowd to speak, let alone give up his confederate.

As we left the cell, O'Dowd spoke for the first time, "I think you will have a devil of a time proving I was on Merlin's Mound, let alone that I killed anyone."

After that he lapsed back into silence. Holmes, Lestrade and I met in one of the small offices.

"He won't help us," said Holmes, "and we have nothing to use as leverage. Take him up to London tomorrow, but keep him isolated as best you can. Make sure that nothing gets into the press. And Lestrade, do not leave until noon, I may wish to interrogate O'Dowd one more time."

"I have four men arriving in the morning to help me escort Mr. O'Dowd," said Lestrade. "But while we are going to London, what is it that you and Dr. Watson will be doing?"

Holmes looked at Lestrade and said simply, "Trying to bring a second murderer to justice."

Chapter 27

The next morning, Holmes and I traveled to the Bath City Science, Art, and Technical School. A relatively new college, it had been formed to foster an interest in the sciences on the part of the area's young people. Holmes was hopeful that we might find a member of the faculty familiar with ogham.

As luck would have it, we were soon directed to a Professor John Coughlin. A genial man, Coughlin was intent upon preserving the histories and literature of the British Isles. In addition to Middle and Old English, he was also familiar with Gaelic and had recently undertaken the study of Welsh.

After sitting at his desk for some 10 minutes, Coughlin looked at us and said, "I can translate it gentlemen, but I cannot make sense of some of it."

"What does it say?" asked Holmes.

"The first two words are easy, it says 'tomorrow night,' but it is the last word that puzzles me."

"And why is that?" inquired Holmes.

"Because it appears that the final word is *tenus*, Latin for 'down'."

"Curious," said Holmes, "a code within a code. Well, I can't thank you enough Professor."

"My pleasure, Mr. Holmes. I just wish I could have been more precise in my efforts."

"Might I impose upon you for one more favor?" asked Holmes.

"Certainly," replied Coughlin, and Holmes then told him exactly what he wanted. I could see the pieces of my friend's plan coming together, and I could only marvel at his ingenuity.

We took a cab back to the station where O'Dowd was being held.

After speaking with Lestrade, Holmes and I went back to the cell so that we could speak with the prisoner. "Good morning, Mr. O'Dowd. In case you were wondering, we managed to translate your note. It appears that you will miss your assignation this evening."

The hatred on O'Dowd's face manifested itself in an angry sneer, but still he remained silent.

"However, I was hoping that you might clear up minor point. Why in the middle of the message do we have the Latin word *tenus?*"

All of a sudden O'Dowd broke his silence by laughing. Holmes looked at him and said, "Thank you again, Mr. O'Dowd. You have confirmed my suspicions."

As we were leaving, O'Dowd began to hurl a string of invectives at Holmes. When we had re-entered the office with Lestrade, Holmes said, "You may take him away, Inspector. Please be careful not to let him escape. He is a very dangerous man and will seize upon the slightest opportunity."

Holding up a pair of shackles that included both handcuffs and leg irons, Lestrade said, "Unless he's been studying under that Houdini chap in America that I've read about, he'll not be getting out of these."

"Just be careful all the same," cautioned Holmes.

When we had left the station, I looked at Holmes and said, "What's next?"

"Tenus," he laughed. "I might have missed it but for O'Dowd's laughter."

"Missed what?"

"It's not one word, but two – ten us."

"And that helps us how? I still don't understand what the difference is between *tenus* and ten us."

"Remember the rest of the message, 'Tomorrow night – ten us. She wanted to meet him at ten o'clock."

"What has the 'us' to do with it?"

`   "I would suggest that you consider the 'us' as a form of shorthand."

"Usual spot," I exclaimed.

"Bravo, Watson. Unfortunately, we have no idea where their usual meeting place is, so then I think we must force the issue and pay a visit to Lady Deveron this afternoon."

After a rather brief lunch at the Saracens Head, Holmes and I hired a cab to take us to Ravenhurst. When we arrived at the estate, the gatekeeper asked if we were expected. Holmes told him that we were not, but that it was a matter of the utmost urgency regarding Her Ladyship's stepson.

There must have been something in Holmes' tone of voice, for the gatekeeper admitted us, albeit reluctantly. "I hope it doesn't cost me my job," he complained.

Holmes ignored the man, and we proceeded to the main house. When we had knocked on the door, we were greeted by a different servant. Holmes handed the man an envelope and said, "Please give this to your mistress. We will wait for an answer."

It must have been at least 15 minutes before the door was opened, and the footman announced, "Her Ladyship will see you."

He led us on a familiar route to the sitting room on the second floor. After we had been seated, we waited another five minutes for Lady Deveron to enter the room. She was followed by another servant wheeling a tea cart.

Upon her entrance, we rose, and Holmes said, "I would like to thank you for seeing us, Lady Deveron."

She looked at Holmes with a withering glance, held up the note and said, "What choice did I have? I don't suppose that I can interest either of you in tea?"

When we shook our heads, she then poured herself a cup, added a lemon wedge and took a tiny sip.

"It's an excellent Darjeeling," she offered. Both Holmes and I again refused her offer.

Holmes steered the conversation back to the subject and said to Lady Deveron, "To answer your question of a moment ago, at the risk of sounding impertinent, you had no choice but to see us. After all, you know an arrest is imminent. How much of a spectacle you wish to make …," Holmes let the words trail off and hang in the air.

"And you think you know everything?" she asked, holding up the note again.

"I know enough to send you and Liam O'Dowd to the gallows," said Holmes. "But I thought I might give you the opportunity to make a statement to me rather than the police."

"What should I say, Mr. Holmes? That my stepson was a beast with absolutely no regard for the feelings of others?"

"He seemed well-liked at school," replied Holmes.

"Anyone with enough money can find friends of a sort," she replied drily. "Trent was cruel and filled with hatred. He blamed me for usurping his father's affection. He blamed me for everything in his life. If he failed an examination, he blamed me. If he couldn't win a young lady's affections, that too was my fault."

"But you killed him," said Holmes.

"And I would do it again," she said.

"But what of the other victims? What did they do to deserve death?"

"Surely, you don't believe that all lives are equal, Mr. Holmes. Consider your towering intellect. Isn't your life, with that amazing brain, worth more than some poor beggar in the East End?"

"That's not for me to judge," replied Holmes firmly.

"My stepson never tired of telling me that the money in our family came from his father, not me. He also delighted in informing me that on the day he reached his majority, I was to pack my bags and leave.

"I had helped raise him, Mr. Holmes, and he was treating me as though I were some poor relation come begging for assistance. I loved his father and he loved me. That is not what he would have wanted, I can assure you."

"What was the source of the boy's enmity?" asked Holmes.

"He came home from school unexpectedly one weekend, and caught Liam and me in a rather compromising position. Since that time, his hatred for me has known no bounds."

"So you determined to kill him, and hoped to have his death attributed to a cult of modern-day druids." Lady Deveron nodded. "Whose idea was it to kill the others?" asked Holmes.

"We had to conceal it, don't you see? I gave Liam orders to find other victims who were a burden on society. I readily admit to being a believer in the principles espoused by Thomas Malthus. That trollop of a girl heading for Canada, what had she ever done that was worthwhile? I give thousands of pounds to charity every year to help the sick and the indigent. That simpleton from Uffington – again, I ask, what had he ever done that was worth remembering?"

"Perhaps they had done nothing – yet," replied Holmes, "but who knows what they might have accomplished as they grew into maturity? Now, because of your avarice, we will never know."

"You're as soft as the rest of them," she wailed. "But I tell you, I will not stand trial and be judged by my peers." As she said this, she quickly poured herself another cup of tea, adding two spoons of sugar and milk, and began to drink.

"Watson, stop her," yelled Holmes. Even as I sprang across the room, she had downed the second cup and then collapsed. She began to convulse and then appeared to go into shock.

Bending down next to me, Holmes said, "Do you smell it, Watson?"

At that point, I detected the faint aroma of bitter almonds in the air. I looked at Holmes and said, "Prussic acid."

He nodded and said, "It's not quite what Dante had in mind, but it is a suitable form of *contrapasso*, don't you think?"

Chapter 28

Rarely did we ever have any sort of collegial gathering at Baker Street, but I prevailed upon Holmes to bring everyone together who had played a role in the case for dinner one evening. Although he was reluctant, I convinced him that telling the story once to a group would preclude him from having to repeat it over and over to all and sundry. "They will help spread the news for you," I assured him.

And so it was that some ten days later, Holmes and I played host to Lestrade, Professor Connors, and Doctors Jeffrey Brewitt and Stephen Smith. Mrs. Hudson had prepared an outstanding meal of Cornish game hens with wild rice. After the meal, Holmes opened a bottle of Armagnac and over brandy and cigars, he began to recount the tale, taking questions as he went.

"Whom did you first suspect?" asked Doctor Brewitt.

"My initial thoughts were that Annie Lock's young swain had murdered her, perhaps out of jealousy, perhaps because she was leaving him. However, after speaking with him, I was convinced that he lacked the guile, and the stomach, to plan and execute such a crime."

"So did you initially then think it was a druidic cabal?" asked Doctor Smith.

"Actually, no," replied Holmes.

"And why is that?" asked Lestrade.

"There are two reasons," said Holmes. "The first is that everything about the murder scene looked rather theatrical. The druidic symbol and the ogham message written in blood, the evisceration and placement of the organs, surrounding the body and the various branches. All of those take time. Most murderers want to kill and be done with it.

"Also, despite my inquiries as well as those of Watson, and a few made by my brother Mycroft's agents, no one had heard even a whisper of a secret society of modern druids."

"But that doesn't mean they don't exist," said Smith.

"No, but you know as well as I that you cannot prove a negative. However, there's an old axiom, I believe it was the American inventor and statesman Benjamin Franklin, who opined, 'Three may keep a secret, if two are dead.'

"I found it difficult, no make that impossible, to believe that such a society could move freely about the country, killing at will, and then vanishing without even a hint of its existence for three months at a time.

"As Doctor Watson will tell you, one of my favorite maxims is, 'When you have eliminated the impossible, whatever remains, however improbable, must be the truth.' Having discarded the druid idea, I began to search for a motive. I could find no reason for anyone to kill Annie Lock. She had no enemies here and few friends; moreover, she was leaving the country. I began to suspect there was some larger plan in motion.

"When Jeremy Mason was killed in the same manner, I saw the pattern, but there was nothing I could pinpoint. Mason was an outlier in his own village. Again, no close friends and no real enemies, but now I had two senseless deaths on my hands."

"Did you suspect Lady Deveron right away after the third murder?" Connors wanted to know.

"Not immediately," replied Holmes, "but as we were leaving Ravenhurst, I was struck by a painting – or should I say the absence of one – in her long gallery."

"I had meant to ask you about that," I said, "but I had quite forgotten."

Holmes smiled at me and said, "Her Ladyship had one of the finest art collections in all of England. As we were departing Ravenhurst, I noticed that one of the paintings looked newer than the others."

"How could an Old Master look newer?" asked Brewitt.

"I misspoke there," said Holmes. "As we walked down the gallery, I observed a border of fresh paint around a portrait. Thinking it odd, I began to examine it more closely. It wasn't fresh paint, but paint that had been hidden from the sun because a slightly larger painting had hung there previously, thus it had not faded as the paint around it had. I also took rough measurements with my walking stick.

"After making some inquiries, I learned that 'A Converted British Family Sheltering a Christian Missionary from the Persecution of the Druids' by William Holmes Hunt had been donated to the Ashmolean Museum of Art and Archaeology in Oxford just five months prior. A quick trip there confirmed that it was just about the size of the painting that had been removed."

And then it hit me. I said, "Lady Deveron had the painting hanging on her wall, but she didn't want anything connected to the druids in her home so she donated it to the museum anonymously – some time before the third murder."

"You hit the mark, Watson!" said Holmes.

"But surely the painting was just the beginning," said Connors.

"Indeed," said Holmes. "So I set about to learn the value of Her Ladyship's holdings, and they are quite considerable. When I learned that she and her stepson were not on the best of terms, I had the beginning of a motive, but I still needed more information.

"I began to look into her background. I discovered that she was originally from Ireland, and I soon found out she was from Donegal. A few well-placed wires informed me that she had been romantically involved with one Liam O'Dowd in her youth, but that her father had broken it off. It seems that he considered O'Dowd beneath his daughter.

"Having now picked up O'Dowd's trail, I learned that he left Donegal determined to make a name for himself and prove her father wrong. Unable to find work, he eventually enlisted in the *Legion Etrangere.*"

"The French Foreign Legion," exclaimed Lestrade. "That would certainly explain his skill with a knife."

"He subsequently saw action in Indochina and fought in the Battle of Hoa Mac. At any rate, he mustered out of the Legion a few years ago, and I'm guessing here – something I am loath to do – but he had apparently kept track of Lady Deveron and since she was a widow, they were free to resume their relationship."

"The only impediment being her stepson," said Connors.

"Yes, the rancor between them could never be reconciled, so they set about devising a plan to eliminate the boy."

"That is monstrous enough, but then to kill other innocent people in an effort to divert suspicion that is beyond the pall," said Smith.

"I quite agree," said Holmes. "I cannot say for certain which one hatched the idea, but when this case was first brought to my attention, I told Watson that I felt the presence of a truly malevolent force at work."

"Were you ever able to link them conclusively before the arrest of O'Dowd?" asked Brewitt.

"Conclusively, no. However, Lady Deveron did call upon Watson and me when she proposed offering a reward for son's death. I suspected that O'Dowd might be in the vicinity, so I had one of my Irregulars, Wiggins, watch her carriage when she arrived and departed. He informed me that when she left our rooms, the door was opened from within by a man using his left hand. At that point, I was certain I was on the right trail and it just became an issue of running the quarry to ground."

"But why offer a reward at all?" asked Connors.

"A ploy designed to reinforce her innocence. And as an added benefit, she and O'Dowd then sent letters designed to misdirect myself and Scotland Yard."

"Sounds like they were a bit too smart for their own good," observed Lestrade.

"Had they chosen their first two victims more carefully, they might well have gotten away with it," said Holmes.

"I don't think so," said Lestrade.

"Oh, why's that?" asked Holmes.

"Because," Lestrade said earnestly, "there's plenty of clever prisoners in Newgate and serving sentences in other jails, both here and abroad, but they are there because there's only one Sherlock Holmes, and I'd wager he's smarter than the lot of 'em put together."

Realizing the sincerity of Lestrade's words and uncertain how to react, Holmes remained silent, as the five of us cheered, "Here, here." I must confess that it is one of the few times I have ever seen my friend rendered utterly speechless.

Author's notes

Almost all of the sites mentioned in this book are real and may be visited. I have also tried to use the names of inns and other establishments that Holmes and Watson might have patronized. Modern readers will appreciate the fact that while you can no longer meander through the slabs at Stonehenge, in Holmes' time, there were no such restrictions.

However, it should be noted that, to the best of my knowledge, there is no estate in England called Ravenhurst.

A number of the people mentioned are real as well, including the Rev. Sabine Baring-Gould, a most interesting individual, whose grandson would go on to pen "Sherlock Holmes of Baker Street: A Life of the World's First Consulting Detective" as well as the two-volume "The Annotated Sherlock Holmes," which has become a standard reference for any serious Sherlockian. Perhaps there is more to the notion of "art in the blood" then we realize.

Most of the other characters, including Lady Judith Deveron and Liam O'Dowd, are the products of my own poor imagination.

If there are errors in the book, I apologize, but they are entirely my fault and cannot be laid at the feet of anyone else.

Acknowledgements

Although the book is dedicated to her, I would not have gotten through it without the incredible patience and support of my wife, Grace. I know that she has far more faith in me than I do in myself, and I thank her for never wavering.

Others who freely provided aid and comfort of all sorts include my brother, Edward; my sister, Arlene; my stalwart publisher, Steve Emecz; and the incredibly talented, cover designer, Brian Belanger.

I am indebted to a number of Sherlockians, including Robert Katz, Fran and Richard Kitts, Ira Matetsky, David Marcum and Marcia Wilson for allowing me to bother them with my questions and taking the time to research, in some cases, and provide me with answers. In truth, their patience rivals that of Holmes.

I should like to thank all my former students for their support and encouragement.

Kudos as well to the staff of the Ashmolean Museum of Art and Archaeology in Oxford, who answered my questions about the painting "A Converted British Family Sheltering a Christian Missionary from the Persecution of the Druids."

Also, a tip of the cap to Stephen Foster, who provided me with some much needed local knowledge about Dartmoor and its environs and to Deborah Annakin Peters for helping with any number of things British.

There are far too many people to thank – the list would be longer than the book – but I should be terribly remiss if I omitted Lauren Esposito, who started me on this journey several years ago. All I can say is, "What a long, strange trip, it's been."

Read on for an excerpt from the newest Sherlock Holmes adventure

by Richard T. Ryan – *The Merchant of Menace*

Coming soon from MX Publishing

The Merchant of Menace –
Introduction

With plenty of time on my hands, having retired after nearly 40 years as a journalist, I have been indulging my passion for the printed word, both reading and writing. Like Holmes, I consider myself a "voracious reader," although my memory is not nearly as sharp as his.

One day as I was rummaging through the various cases in the tin dispatch box of Dr. Watson that I had acquired in Scotland, I noticed that the bottom seemed ever so slightly uneven. Upon a closer examination, I realized that what I thought was the bottom of the case was actually a thin piece of metal that had been cut to the exact dimensions of the box. Taking a screwdriver, I was able to pry up that false bottom, and I came across this latest case, which oddly enough, had been hidden there.

I found the notion of Watson secreting a manuscript away in the bottom of a box which he owned, and which many believed to be residing in the vaults of Cox and Company, too fascinating to resist.

As readers of past efforts know, the cases in this box had all been withheld from the public for various reasons, and "The Merchant of Menace" was no exception. While Holmes' vanity forestalled the publication of "The Druid of Death," and the potential political fallout precluded the publication of "The Vatican Cameos" and to a lesser degree, "The Stone of Destiny," I can come up with no such compelling reason for withholding this particular manuscript, let alone hiding it, save perhaps the embarrassment that it might have caused had it been released.

However, after re-reading Watson's notes, I finally came to understand his reticence. I can only think that this particular case did not see the light of day because of the good doctor's misgivings about its publication and his sense of propriety. That bit of information having been dispensed with, I caution readers that this is one of the strangest cases that ever found its way to 221b Baker Street.

If, like the Great Detective, you have a taste for the *outre,* then I think you will find this tale to your liking. If nothing else, it certainly offers an insight into the sensibilities of the Edwardian era that Holmes called home.

Richard T. Ryan

Chapter 1: London, 1906

This case, which proved to be a true test of the mettle of Sherlock Holmes, began innocently enough.

One morning while reading the paper over breakfast, an item captured my attention. According to the Guardian, a rare, jewel-encrusted dagger had been stolen from the library of Lord William Thornton. Thinking that my friend might find this of interest, I asked, "Holmes, have you read about the theft of this dagger?"

"Indeed, I have," he replied. "Probably some footman pilfered it in order to settle his gambling debts. There is nothing there for us, I believe."

I wasn't surprised at my friend's lack of enthusiasm. Common crimes did little to stimulate his interest, and truth be told, he found them more tiresome than challenging. However, having warmed to the subject, he continued, "Moreover, I must say that people who keep such *objects d'art* around the house are just asking for trouble. Decorations are one thing, but a trophy such as that, acquired only because you are wealthy, well, that just strikes me as rather ostentatious."

"You can't mean that," I said. "Look at your own collection of odds and ends that litter our lodgings."

"Yes, but none of my possessions, strange and varied as they may be, was looted from a foreign country." Sweeping his arm about the room, he said, "There is nothing here that has not been earned and paid for by the sweat of my brow."

"Does that include your Stradivarius?"

Ignoring my jibe, Holmes continued, "At any rate, I am expecting a visit from Lestrade regarding that self-same dagger."

"And what will you tell him?"

"Look to the servants," replied my friend. "They are always among us and yet they are seldom noticed."

Thinking those were the traits of any good person in service, I returned to my paper as Holmes resumed working on a monograph that he was preparing regarding tattoos and the criminal element. Perhaps an hour later, just as I was preparing to leave for my club, I heard the bell ring.

"I shouldn't be surprised if that were Lestrade now," said Holmes.

I decided to wait, and a moment later, there was a knock on the door. "Come in, Mrs. Hudson," my friend yelled across the room.

Our landlady entered and said, "There is a gentleman here to see you, Mr. Holmes."

I could see by the look on his face that Holmes was genuinely surprised – and pleased. "Please show him up, Mrs. Hudson." Looking at me he said, "A new client and perhaps a visit from Lestrade – this has all the makings of a truly exceptional day."

A moment later, a tall, spare gentleman with close-cropped gray hair stepped into our rooms. After examining us both, he turned to where Holmes was seated and said in a deep, sonorous voice, "Mr. Holmes, I am Lord William Thornton. Perhaps you have heard of me?" he continued as he handed Holmes his card.

"I have heard of your missing dagger, and by extension, yourself," my friend replied.

"I had rather hoped to keep the theft a secret, but apparently such things are impossible once the law is involved."

"And with whom have you spoken from Scotland Yard? Inspector Lestrade?"

"Yes. In fact, Inspector Lestrade has arrested my butler and charged him with the theft."

Glancing at me with an I-told-you-so-look on his face, Holmes replied, "If an arrest has been made, then why are you here?"

"Johnson, my butler, has been with me for more than 20 years. He would no more have taken that dagger than you, Mr. Holmes."

"Do tell. Then why did Lestrade arrest him? Surely, he had evidence of some sort in order to justify the charge."

"They found a large sum of money in Johnson's room, and after some inquiries they learned that he also owed more than a three hundred pounds to a bookmaker."

After another glance in my direction, Holmes said, "I grant you that the evidence is circumstantial, but on the surface it does seem rather convincing, does it not? What does your man say for himself?"

"He admits to being in debt," said Thornton.

"And how does he explain the money?" asked Holmes.

"He refuses to say where the money came from."

"Curious," said Holmes. "A simple explanation might free him, but he allows himself to be arrested instead.

"Did anyone else have access to the dagger?"

223

"Many people did," replied Thornton. "The night before it was discovered missing we had a small gathering at the house to celebrate my wife's birthday."

"When you say 'small,' exactly how many people are we talking about?"

"There were four other couples, but they are all above suspicion."

"No one is above suspicion, Lord Thornton. People will do the most unexpected things for reasons that defy any type of rational explanation. May I ask where the dagger came from and where it was kept?"

"My father was an officer in the army during the first Opium War, and he brought the dagger back from China. He would never say exactly how the weapon had come into his possession, and since he's been dead for seven years, I suppose we'll never know how he came by it. However, he was inordinately fond of it to the point where he had a special wooden holder constructed in order to display the dagger. He always kept it on his desk. Since his passing, I have done the same."

"Interesting," said Holmes. "One is always curious about the provenance of such items, and whether they actually belong to their owners."

"What are you suggesting?" asked Thornton angrily.

"I am merely pointing out that we know precious little about the object in question. While it has been in your family for these many years, there may be others who believe that the dagger is rightfully theirs."

"Possession is nine-tenths of the law," replied Thornton.

"If you are going to quote legal axioms, at least quote them correctly," said Holmes.

"I beg your pardon?"

"The actual saying is that 'possession is nine points of the law' and if you wish to trace that maxim to its Scottish origins, they hold that 'possession is eleven points of the law and there be but twelve.' But we are digressing.

"The people at your soiree, friends and business acquaintances?" asked Holmes.

"All close friends of long duration, and I would be willing to swear that none of them took the dagger."

At that point, there was a knock on the door. "Yes, Mrs. Hudson?" asked Holmes.

Poking her head inside the door, she announced, "Inspector Lestrade is here to see you, Mr. Holmes."

"By all means, show him up."

I could see that Holmes was enjoying the idea of Lestrade in the same room with Thornton. "Are you sure this is wise?" I whispered after Thornton had turned to the door.

"We are all civilized," replied Holmes. "Good afternoon, Inspector. What brings you here today?"

As soon as Lestrade had entered the room, he caught sight of Thornton. "I have questions about a case," replied the Inspector.

Looking at Thornton, Lestrade said, "Lord Thornton, may I remind you that I am the investigating officer on your case. Any concerns that you have should be addressed to me. There's no need to involve Mr. Holmes, here."

"I told you that Johnson was innocent, but you arrested him anyway," replied Thornton. "I will not stand idly by while there is a grave miscarriage of justice."

"I did not arrest Mr. Johnson," replied Lestrade evenly. "I merely detained him at the Yard so that I could question him. He has answered all my questions satisfactorily. His story has been verified, and he has been released."

"Well, Inspector," said Thornton, "have you recovered the dagger?"

"Not yet," replied Lestrade, "but I have my best men working on it."

"By the way, Inspector, may I inquire as to what occasioned your visit to Mr. Holmes?" asked Thornton.

"That's police business. Another case entirely," replied Lestrade.

"Inspector, I shall give you a limited time to recover the dagger." Turning to my friend, he continued, "Mr. Holmes, if the dagger is not in my possession by that time, I should like to retain you to ascertain its whereabouts."

"Let us cross that bridge when we come to it, Mr. Thornton. I have your card. Here is mine. Should anything else about the dagger or the theft occur to you, please inform Inspector Lestrade. Should the need arise, I will consult with him."

"Thank you, Mr. Holmes," he said, shaking my friend's hand. Looking at myself and then Lestrade, he said, "Dr. Watson, Inspector, a good day to you both."

After he had left, Holmes looked at Lestrade and said, "Another case entirely? Prevarication hardly suits you, Inspector."

"I had to tell him something Mr. Holmes. The man has been making my life miserable. If I didn't know better, I'd swear he had something to hide himself."

"So you have come about the dagger?"

Looking sheepish, Lestrade said, "I do need your help Mr. Holmes. When we had the butler down at the Yard, he admitted that the money had been given to him by Thornton's wife. When I braced her about it, she admitted loaning Johnson the money and begged me not to tell her husband. You may make of that what you will, but I was rather impressed by the man's nobility."

"That's all well and good, Lestrade, but what have you learned concerning the theft?"

"That's the problem, Mr. Holmes. All of Thornton's guests and their spouses were together the night of the theft. No one remembers anyone leaving the room for any length of time. Three of the four couples are better off than he, and the remaining couple isn't wanting for anything, either."

"So, we have a stolen dagger that was taken at an unseen time by a person or persons unknown," said Holmes.

"That about sums it up," said Lestrade.

Turning to me, Holmes smiled and said, "Watson, perhaps I was mistaken in my initial assessment of the crime. There may be something of interest here yet."

"So then you'll help me, Mr. Holmes?" asked Lestrade.

"Indeed. I shall also try to be as discreet as possible. After all, you know how much those thieves from the spectral realm hate being disturbed."

I saw Lestrade redden slightly, but since he was in need of my friend's help, he remained silent.

Also from Richard T Ryan

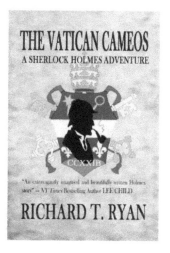

When the papal apartments are burgled in 1901, Sherlock Holmes is summoned to Rome by Pope Leo XII. After learning from the pontiff that several priceless cameos that could prove compromising to the church, and perhaps determine the future of the newly unified Italy, have been stolen, Holmes is asked to recover them. In a parallel story, Michelangelo, the toast of Rome in 1501 after the unveiling of his Pieta, is commissioned by Pope Alexander VI, the last of the Borgia pontiffs, with creating the cameos that will bedevil Holmes and the papacy four centuries later. For fans of Conan Doyle's immortal detective, the game is always afoot. However, the great detective has never encountered an adversary quite like the one with whom he crosses swords in "The Vatican Cameos."

"An extravagantly imagined and beautifully written Holmes story"
(**Lee Child**, NY Times Bestselling author, Jack Reacher series)

What none of us failed to realize at the time was just how prophetic Holmes' words would prove to be.

Also from Richard T Ryan

During the elaborate funeral for Queen Victoria, a group of Irish separatists breaks into Westminster Abbey and steals the Coronation Stone, on which every monarch of England has been crowned since the 14th century. After learning of the theft from Mycroft, Sherlock Holmes is tasked with recovering the stone and returning it to England. In pursuit of the many-named stone, which has a rich and colorful history, Holmes and Watson travel to Ireland in disguise as they try to infiltrate the Irish Republican Brotherhood, the group they believe responsible for the theft. The story features a number of historical characters, including a very young Michael Collins, who would go on to play a prominent role in Irish history; John Theodore Tussaud, the grandson of Madame Tussaud; and George Bradley, the dean of Westminster at the time of the theft. There are also references to a number of other Victorian luminaries, including Joseph Lister and Frederick Treves.

Also from MX Publishing

MX Publishing is the world's largest specialist Sherlock Holmes publisher, with over a hundred titles and fifty authors creating the latest in Sherlock Holmes fiction and non-fiction.

From traditional short stories and novels to travel guides and quiz books, MX Publishing cater for all Holmes fans.

The collection includes leading titles such as *Benedict Cumberbatch In Transition* and *The Norwood Author* which won the 2011 Howlett Award (Sherlock Holmes Book of the Year).

MX Publishing also has one of the largest communities of Holmes fans on Facebook with regular contributions from dozens of authors.

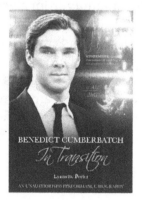

www.mxpublishing.com

Also from MX Publishing

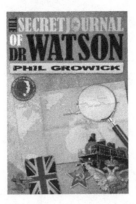

"Phil Growick's, 'The Secret Journal of Dr Watson', is an adventure which takes place in the latter part of Holmes and Watson's lives. They are entrusted by HM Government (although not officially) and the King no less to undertake a rescue mission to save the Romanovs, Russia's Royal family from a grisly end at the hand of the Bolsheviks. There is a wealth of detail in the story but not so much as would detract us from the enjoyment of the story. Espionage, counter-espionage, the ace of spies himself, double-agents, double-crossers...all these flit across the pages in a realistic and exciting way. All the characters are extremely well-drawn and Mr Growick, most importantly, does not falter with a very good ear for Holmesian dialogue indeed. Highly recommended. A five-star effort."
The Baker Street Society

www.mxpublishing.com

Also from MX Publishing

The Missing Authors Series

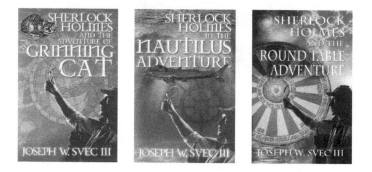

Sherlock Holmes and The Adventure of The Grinning Cat
Sherlock Holmes and The Nautilus Adventure
Sherlock Holmes and The Round Table Adventure

"Joseph Svec, III is brilliant in entwining two endearing and enduring classics of literature, blending the factual with the fantastical; the playful with the pensive; and the mischievous with the mysterious. We shall, all of us young and old, benefit with a cup of tea, a tranquil afternoon, and a copy of Sherlock Holmes, The Adventure of the Grinning Cat."
Amador County Holmes Hounds Sherlockian Society

Also from MX Publishing

The American Literati Series

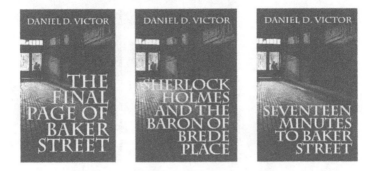

The Final Page of Baker Street
The Baron of Brede Place
Seventeen Minutes To Baker Street

"The really amazing thing about this book is the author's ability to call up the 'essence' of both the Baker Street 'digs' of Holmes and Watson as well as that of the 'mean streets' of Marlowe's Los Angeles. Although none of the action takes place in either place, Holmes and Watson share a sense of camaraderie and self-confidence in facing threats and problems that also pervades many of the later tales in the Canon. Following their conversations and banter is a return to Edwardian England and its certainties and hope for the future. This is definitely the world before The Great War."
Philip K Jones

Also from MX Publishing

The Detective and The Woman Series

The Detective and The Woman
The Detective, The Woman and The Winking Tree
The Detective, The Woman and The Silent Hive

"The book is entertaining, puzzling and a lot of fun. I believe the author has hit on the only type of long-term relationship possible for Sherlock Holmes and Irene Adler. The details of the narrative only add force to the romantic defects we expect in both of them and their growth and development are truly marvelous to watch. This is not a love story. Instead, it is a coming-of-age tale starring two of our favorite characters."
Philip K Jones

www.mxpublishing.com

235

Also from MX Publishing

The Sherlock Holmes and Enoch Hale Series

The Amateur Executioner
The Poisoned Penman
The Egyptian Curse

"The Amateur Executioner: Enoch Hale Meets Sherlock Holmes", the first collaboration between Dan Andriacco and Kieran McMullen, concerns the possibility of a Fenian attack in London. Hale, a native Bostonian, is a reporter for London's Central News Syndicate - where, in 1920, Horace Harker is still a familiar figure, though far from revered. "The Amateur Executioner" takes us into an ambiguous and murky world where right and wrong aren't always distinguishable. I look forward to reading more about Enoch Hale."
Sherlock Holmes Society of London

www.mxpublishing.com

Also from MX Publishing

Sherlock Holmes novellas in verse

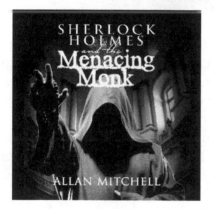

All four novellas
have been
released also in
audio format
with narration
by Steve White

Sherlock Holmes and The Menacing Moors
Sherlock Holmes and The Menacing Metropolis
Sherlock Holmes and The Menacing Melbournian
Sherlock Holmes and The Menacing Monk

"The story is really good and the Herculean effort it must have been to write it all in verse—well, my hat is off to you, Mr. Allan Mitchell! I wouldn't dream of seeing such work get less than five plus stars from me..." **The Raven**

Also from MX Publishing

The Conan Doyle Notes (The Hunt For Jack The Ripper)
"Holmesians have long speculated on the fact that the Ripper murders aren't mentioned in the canon, though the obvious reason is undoubtedly the correct one: even if Conan Doyle had suspected the killer's identity he'd never have considered mentioning it in the context of a fictional entertainment. Ms Madsen's novel equates his silence with that of the dog in the night-time, assuming that Conan Doyle did know who the Ripper was but chose not to say – which, of course, implies that good old stand-by, the government cover-up. It seems unlikely to me that the Ripper was anyone famous or distinguished, but fiction is not fact, and "The Conan Doyle Notes" is a gripping tale, with an intelligent, courageous and very likable protagonist in DD McGil."
The Sherlock Holmes Society of London

www.mxpublishing.com

"The Vatican Cameos opens with a familiar feel for fans of Arthur Conan Doyle's original Sherlock Holmes stories. The plotting is clever, and the alternating stories well-told." – Crime Thriller Hound

"A masterful spin on the ageless Sherlock Holmes. Somewhere I'm certain Sir Arthur Conan Doyle himself is standing and cheering" – Jake Needham, author of the Jack Sheperd and Inspector Samuel Tay series

Paperback ISBN 978-1-78705-294-9
Hardcover ISBN 978-1-78705-295-6
ePub ISBN 978-1-78705-296-3
PDF ISBN 978-1-78705-297-0

Published in the UK by MX Publishing
335 Princess Park Manor, Royal Drive,
London, N11 3GX
www.mxpublishing.com

Cover design by Brian Belanger.

"The Stone of Destiny"

"Sometimes a book comes along that absolutely restores your faith in reading. Such is the 'found manuscript of Dr. Watson, 'The Stone of Destiny.' Exhilarating, superb narrative and a cast of characters that are as dark as they are vivid. ... A thriller of the very first rank." – Ken Bruen, author of "The Guards," "The Magdalen Martyrs" and many other novels, as well as the creator of the Jack Taylor character

"Somewhere Sir Arthur Conan Doyle is smiling. Ryan's 'The Stone of Destiny' is a fine addition to the Canon." – Reed Farrel Coleman, New York Times Bestselling author of "What You Break"

"A wonderful read for both the casual Sherlock Holmes fan and the most die-hard devotees of the beloved character." – Terrence McCauley, author of "A Conspiracy of Ravens" and "A Murder of Crows"

"Full of interesting facts, the story satisfies and may even have you believing that Holmes and Watson actually existed." — Crime Thriller Hound

"Ryan's Holmes is the real deal in ['The Stone of Destiny.'] One hopes the author is hard at work on the next adventure in this wonderfully imagined and executed series." – Fran Wood, What Fran's Reading for nj.com

The Druid of Death:
A Sherlock Holmes
Adventure

By Richard T. Ryan

reader must make for himself. To that end, I have provided a copy of the doctor's letter, and I leave it the individual reader to decide whether to press on and read the tale or to heed the wishes of Holmes.

As I said, I find myself siding with the doctor, and my decision is rendered with a genuine tenderness for Holmes and the honest belief that at least in this one instance, Holmes' vanity would deprive readers of an otherwise excellent adventure that I believe shows him at the absolute top of his game.

I think, had the Great Detective enjoyed the advantage of hindsight that we enjoy as well as the objectivity that we can bring to bear on this tale, he might have been persuaded to change his mind.

At any rate, here is the tale, preceded by Doctor Watson's missive. I hope you enjoy both, but I will certainly understand, if after perusing the letter, you should decide not to read the book.

Richard T. Ryan

Introduction

Those who have read either one of the previous stories that have appeared under my name are familiar with the origins of the manuscripts. While on a golfing holiday in Scotland, I attended an estate sale where I emerged victorious, after a rather spirited bidding war, as the owner of a locked box.

Upon forcing it open, I discovered a second box inside the first. Equally surprising was the fact that stenciled on the lid of the second box was the name "John H. Watson." Indeed, it was the famed tin dispatch box of Sherlock Holmes' friend and companion. Moreover, it was filled with manuscripts that had failed to see the light of day for various reasons during the great sleuth's lifetime.

I believe that "The Vatican Cameos" was held back because of the possible political fallout it posed to a newly unified Italy as well as the potential embarrassment its release might have caused the papacy.

"The Stone of Destiny" was never published, I assume, because of the political tension that existed between England and Ireland at the time. I suppose a secondary reason for keeping it hidden might have been the fact that its release might have placed Holmes in a rather precarious position with the powers that be.

With this book, which Watson had titled "The Druid of Death," there can be no doubt as to why the adventure was kept secret. Attached to the folder that contained the manuscript was a letter in the good doctor's handwriting that explained his reticence in making the public aware of the facts.

Having read the entire tale, I find myself in agreement with Watson's assessment; however, that is a judgment that each

As always, this book is dedicated to my wife, Grace, who not only does the impossible on a daily basis but puts up with it as well.

And to my children, Dr. Kate Ryan-Smith and Michael, as well as my son-in-law, Daniel. Each, in his or her own way, is a source of inspiration to me.

Finally, this book is dedicated to the memory of my parents.

9 781787 052949